Uncle Bill

When we say punching cows we mean all the work that goes with handling cattle.

Uncle Bill

A Tale of Two Kids and a Cowboy

BY

WILL JAMES

Illustrated by the Author

MOUNTAIN PRESS PUBLISHING COMPANY
Missoula, Montana
1998

First Printing, June 1998

Mountain Press Publishing Company changed a few words in *Uncle Bill*
that are racially offensive to modern society. Mountain Press made the changes
with the permission of the copyright holder and with the view that many titles
of the Tumbleweed Series are purchased for school libraries and for children.

Library of Congress Cataloging-in-Publication Data

James, Will, 1892–1942.
    Uncle Bill : a tale of two kids and a cowboy / by Will James.
        p.   cm.
    Summary: Ten-year-old Kip and his older sister Scootie spend a summer
at the Five Barb Ranch, where the old cowboy known as Uncle Bill teaches
them to ride and rope and take care of themselves wherever they are in
cow country.
    ISBN 0-87842-380-X (alk. paper). — ISBN 0-87842-379-6 (alk. paper)
    [1. Cowboys–Fiction. 2. Ranch life–Fiction.] I. Title.
PZ7.J545Un   1998
[Fic]–dc21   98-24103
                                                                             CIP
                                                                             AC

PRINTED IN THE U.S.A.

Mountain Press Publishing Company
P.O. Box 2399 • 1301 S. Third Street W.
Missoula, Montana 59806

PUBLISHER'S NOTE

WILL JAMES'S BOOKS represent an American treasure. His writings and drawings introduced generations of captivated readers to the lifestyle and spirit of the American cowboy and the West. Following James's death in 1942, the reputation of this remarkable artist and writer languished, and nearly all of his twenty-four books went out of print. But in recent years, interest in James's work has surged, due in part to the publication of several biographies and film documentaries, public exhibitions of James's art, and the formation of the Will James Society.

Now, in conjunction with the Will James Art Company of Billings, Montana, Mountain Press Publishing Company is reprinting each of Will James's classic books in handsome cloth and paperback editions. The new editions contain all the original artwork and text, feature an attractive new design, and are printed on acid-free paper to ensure many years of reading pleasure. They will be republished under the name the Tumbleweed Series.

The republication of Will James's books would not have been possible without the help and support of the many fans of Will James. Because all James's books and artwork remain under copyright protection, the Will James Art Company has been instrumental in providing the necessary permissions and furnishing artwork. Special care has been taken to keep each volume in the Tumbleweed Series faithful to the original vision of Will James.

Mountain Press is pleased to make Will James's books available again. Read and enjoy!

The Will James Society was formed in 1992 as a nonprofit organization dedicated to preserving the memory and works of Will James. The society is one of the primary catalysts behind a growing interest in not only Will James and his work, but also the life and heritage of the working cowboy. For more information on the society, contact:

Will James Society • c/o Will James Art Company
2237 Rosewyn Lane • Billings, Montana 59102

BOOKS BY WILL JAMES

Cowboys North and South, 1924

The Drifting Cowboy, 1925

Smoky, the Cowhorse, 1926

Cow Country, 1927

Sand, 1929

Lone Cowboy, 1930

Sun Up, 1931

Big Enough, 1931

Uncle Bill, 1932

All in the Day's Riding, 1933

The Three Mustangers, 1933

Home Ranch, 1935

Young Cowboy, 1935

In the Saddle with Uncle Bill, 1935

Scorpion, 1936

Cowboy in the Making, 1937

Flint Spears, 1938

Look-See with Uncle Bill, 1938

The Will James Cowboy Book, 1938

The Dark Horse, 1939

Horses I Have Known, 1940

My First Horse, 1940

The American Cowboy, 1942

Will James Book of Cowboy Stories, 1951

To Scootie

PREFACE

SINCE I BEGIN WRITING, a few years ago, I've had to leave my home range quite a few times, sometimes to discuss things with my publishers in the "big town," and other times to sort of meet up with some of the readers of my writings at book stores of different cities.

That way I got to meeting many folks who'd never seen or heard of the cow country only thru books or movies, and I been asked many questions which sounded strange to me, but they was only natural and no more strange than some I might ask about the city.

I get letters with steady streams of questions, and it's often hard to tell by them wether they're from youngsters or grown ups, because anybody not knowing and wanting information about the range country, the cowboy, riding, roping, handling cattle and horses and taking in the life on the range in general is apt to ask pretty well the same questions wether the person asking is eight or eighty years old.

In this story I'm having a boy and a girl coming west from a big city. They ask many questions and of the kind that's been asked of me often and I'm putting 'em in the care of an old cowboy to answer all their questions. This old cowboy who is called Uncle Bill teaches the kids how to ride and rope and how to be all around good range riders. He tells 'em true range stories of rustlers and gunmen and shows how the most of 'em ain't so bad. He teaches 'em how to camp in the hills, how to take care of their horses and how to take care of themselves wherever they are in the cow country. He takes 'em on big cattle round-ups and coaches 'em in a way where I think the reader will catch on to things near as well by reading as the kids did while on the trail with the old cowboy.

Now I'll let Uncle Bill say "hello" and talk to you.

ILLUSTRATIONS

Uncle Bill

CHAPTER ONE

"IT'S MY TURN now, Kip."

"All right, Scootie, just this once more and then you can have it."

The object for this talk was a forty foot lasso-rope which Kip, a boy of ten was trying to rope a corral post with. He'd been trying hard and with no luck, so far. The loop wouldn't stay open and he had better luck catching his own self with it than he did the post.

He hated to give up the rope till he made at least one catch, but his sister Scootie, a year older than Kip, had her ambitions that way too, and as each throw was counted she wasn't going to let her turn go by without saying a word about it.

It was as the rope was about to change hands that an old cowboy come near and stopped, grinning a bit, to watch the goings on, but his grin sort of faded as he looked at the rope. It was his own and the neat coils had already been twisted out of shape.

At first he was for taking it away from the kids, but somehow he didn't make a step or say a word, and soon he begin to grin again as he watched the pair. He watched 'em take their turns and seen where he'd sure have to get himself a new rope because that one had sure been appropriated and he could never depend on it being on his saddle no more. And so, as he watched the kids, each one anxious and waiting for their turn and getting tangled up with the length of the rope he decided to make the best of it and help 'em out a bit. He took the rope away from 'em, straightened out the kinks, then doubled it and cut it in two. He made another hondoo for another loop and now there was a rope for each and with a length they could handle a lot better.

"How do you throw a rope anyhow, Uncle Bill?" asks Scootie.

"Just throw it, that's all. The only thing is it takes practice, and knack too. Like learning how to play a fiddle for instance, some folks can never learn how to play one and others can pick it up right quick."

The old cowboy took one of the ropes, made a loop, gave it a flip and made a neat catch.

"Gee, that looks easy," says Kip. "But I don't think I'll ever be able to rope like that."

"You can't tell yet, wait till you're here a while."

The rope, the same as the Five Barb ranch where Kip and Scootie was at was all new to them. They'd been at the ranch only one day, and coming from the far away crowded city where they'd been born and raised, the ranch, the wide open country around, and the tall mountains skirting it was mighty strange, mighty interesting, and promising for many a thrill.

And they had that same country to thank for what all was now ahead for them, for there was where their dad had been brought up and where he'd stayed till a college education spoiled him from coming back. He'd took on a business in the city, married there, and when the old man passed away and willed his outfit to him and another son he sold his share and settled down

The old cowboy took one of the ropes, gave it a flip and made a neat catch.

WILLJAMES
'32

to the business he'd started. He was range born but he belonged to the city.

His brother didn't care at all for the city, he'd stayed a bachelor and with the ranch, and as the two brothers kept a writing to one another once a year or so is how come that the city brother received a letter from the ranch brother one spring and was asked to send the two kids out for a summer airing on the ranch.

"I have a good lady cook who will take good care of them while they are inside," it says in the letter, "and a good old cowboy to stand guard on 'em while they're outside. Send 'em on out."

The kids sure didn't need no coaxing to be "sent out." The most open country they'd ever seen was vacant lots full of rubbish, and city parks, but they'd got a faint idea of more open country thru seeing western movies once in a while, just enough so they hankered to see more of it, and when the news was broke to 'em that they was to come West and be on a real ranch they come near not qualifying during the last days before school closed.

Kip and Scootie was sent West in care of the conductor, and after a couple of days of train riding they come to where there was a water tank which come near hiding what there was of a town. They stared wide-eyed as the conductor told 'em they'd come to the end of their ride, and they stared some more when as they stepped down on the platform of the depot they was met by a cowboy, a real cowboy. It was their Uncle Frank.

The sixty mile ride to the ranch was made in a big powerful car, and, with glancing at their uncle and looking at the big country around, it was the first time in their lives they felt they couldn't speak. It was an entirely new world to 'em and they wouldn't of been any more thrilled if they'd been riding over the moon. The long distances with nothing in sight but scattered bunches of cattle and horses, the clear air that made the far away tall mountains look so close, the deep canyons in 'em and all that was for the eye to see, made the tongue keep still. But the tongue wasn't still for so long so it lost any action. Uncle Frank started the talk going, and soon enough the kids limbered up their tongues and asked about as many questions as their uncle could handle.

For steady speed, the questions came about as fast as the car went. There was a steady stream of 'em as they come to a long grade up a mountain, crossed a divide so high that snow was still deep in the road, then down on the other side, acrost a wide valley, over another mountain and around a point of the foothills, to the ranch.

The sight of the long low and scattered ranch buildings, groves of trees, corrals, and many cattle and horses cut the talk short again. It seemed like they couldn't see as well when they talked, and right then they felt that just looking was about all they could do.

Uncle Frank drove the car up to the long porch of the ranch house. The kids jumped out, and while they was helping take their things out of the car a lean gray-headed cowboy came up. It was old Uncle Bill.

Uncle Bill was no real uncle to anybody, he was just as shy of relatives as a terrapin is of feathers. Maybe it was for that reason that everybody in that country called him Uncle Bill, and maybe it was because he was always handing out advice and wise words every chance he got.

The old cowboy had been with the Five-Barb outfit ever since when the two Powers boys was still youngsters. He'd started in at breaking horses for their dad and later kept on the payroll as an all-around hand. There was few better riders and ropers than Bill then and as a cowman he was a wizard. He could near read a brand right thru a critter, and if he seen a horse once he could remember that horse a year afterwards and spot him amongst a thousand others.

Now, his hard riding days was pretty well over. He just sort of tinkered around and kept an eye open for what all he could do. With all his experience he could do a plenty that was valuable to the outfit, even while just tinkering around. He was always riding somewhere amongst the stock, and he got to be just as much part of the Five-Barb range as the cottonwoods and pine that was on it.

It didn't take Kip and Scootie long to get under Uncle Bill's old hide, and Martha, the cook, took them on to herself just as soon as they walked in the house and sort of purred around 'em. The whole ranch seemed to take on a new light, still tongues begin to loosen up and serious faces went to cracking with smiles. Even the cowboys down at the bunk house begin to look towards wherever the kids was at when they rode in that evening, and they listened to the laughing that came down from the ranch house like they would listen to the first meadow lark of spring.

"I'd sure like to taste some of Martha's cooking," says one of the boys, sort of going around what he was aiming at.

"Me, too," says another. "I'd like a change from this ranch cook's grub."

If the cowboys was anxious to talk and joke with the kids they was no more anxious than the kids was, but they didn't get to mix the next day because the cowboys rode away at daybreak and wasn't back till dark. Frank had a talk with Uncle Bill that morning and asked him if he'd take on the job of herding the kids.

Uncle Bill acted sort of grouchy at that. "I ain't no nurse maid," he says, but he felt happy inside.

"I know it ain't in your line," says Frank, grinning, "but all you have to do is sort of keep your weather eye on 'em and see that they don't do anything where they might get hurt. They'll get onto things after a few days and then they won't be so much worry. You can teach 'em how to ride and I don't think you'll mind that."

"I guess not," he says, losing his grouchy look.

THE FIRST THING TO HAPPEN as Uncle Bill turned his back that morning was to see his rope in the kids' hands and getting all kinked up. After he'd cut the rope in two and gave them a few lessons with it he figured it safe to leave 'em alone for a few minutes and till he went to the commissary to get himself a new one, they each had a post and a rope apiece now and they would be practicing making a loop and throwing it the way he'd showed 'em.

And sure enough, they was still at it when he came back and he turned the corner of the bunk house just in time to see Scootie make her first catch. She let out a glad yell at that first catch and it made her double glad as she looked around that Uncle Bill had seen her do it. Kip didn't feel so glad about it, his pride was hurt a bit that a girl, even if she was his sister, beat him at making the first catch. But that didn't discourage him any. If anything it made him all the more determined. He was more careful in judging the distance to the post and in making his loop and after half a dozen more tries he finally made a pretty fair catch.

It was then that Uncle Bill came in with some more lessons in the art of roping. First, and with his new rope he showed 'em how to tie a hondoo. The binding knot looked mighty easy to tie, but the kids didn't get onto how to tie it, not that day. Anyhow they was more interested in how to throw a rope right then, so the old cowboy proceeded to start and teach 'em.

"Now," he says, "don't forget that you ain't throwing a stick or a stone when you throw a rope. You got to get the balance of your loop first whether you have it on or off the ground. If it's on the ground don't jerk it, just sort of drag it off a bit till you get it in the air and till you get the swing of it, and the hondoo ought to be away from your hand and half-ways down the loop to give it good balance.

"There's about a hundred different kinds of throws," he went on. "Most every cowboy knows at least twenty-five of 'em. It all depends wether you're afoot or horseback, standing or running and which way you're roping, just what throw you're going to use, just like when you eat soup or meat, you use a spoon for the soup and a knife for the meat."

You got to get the balance of your loop first.

With his new rope, he showed 'em a dozen different throws, three or four of 'em for catching horses in a corral and a few others for catching horses and

WILL JAMES

9

cattle on the range and while a horseback. He showed 'em that famous throw, the "Johnnie Blocker," a throw where the loop sails out in front of a critter and then doubles back. Then he showed 'em the "figure eight," a mighty hard throw to make and which is used in calf roping, that's where the loop catches the animal by the neck and front feet and crosses under the neck. He showed a few heel throws (hind legs) and front footing (catching horses by the front feet), and all the while the kids stood a staring in wonder. Old Uncle Bill had turned out to be a regular god to 'em.

"You don't have to whirl a loop over your head to catch anything," he says, "not unless you're riding at full speed, you do that then because your rope needs more speed than what you're making yourself, the rope has more breeze to split. But while you're in a corral, riding slow or standing still it's best not to whirl your loop. Some outfits won't allow it, specially when catching horses, because the whirling loop spooks them up and makes 'em run around too much."

A whole lot of the forenoon was spent on the roping education, and by the time the kids' arms got so tired they both had made quite a few catches. They now had a start and knowed how to get a loop in the air without it twisting up. Of course they couldn't do that very well yet but they had an idea how and all they'd need would be practice.

"There's a heap of difference between catching a post and a live dodging animal," says Uncle Bill, as he showed 'em how to coil up their ropes before putting 'em away. "But practicing at a post will help some and after you get fair at that I'll give you two a chance at roping calves, that'll be more fun."

Both Kip and Scootie more than agreed on that last as they followed him to the stables and saddle room. There a new interest came to the top and roping was forgot for the time.

"Gee, those are big saddles," says Kip, as he sighted a few of 'em hanging up. "Don't a horse get tired packing them?"

"No more than with any other saddle, Son. It ain't the saddles that tires a horse, it's the rider, it all depends how you ride. I seen some riders that weighed two hundred pounds that used forty pound saddles that could go further on the same horse without tiring him than some light rider using a light saddle. Our saddles average about thirty pounds, and if they fit a horse's back well they're more of a help to him than a light saddle because the heavy saddle is more of a part of him. It fits him closer at every move him or the rider makes."

"But do they have to be this heavy?" asks Scootie. "The people who ride in the parks at home use small flat saddles."

"Yes, but they're riding in parks and not chasing thru rough hills like out here. Another thing is the most of 'em ride just a few miles day and for exercise, where with us it's work, and what we make our living at. Sometimes on round ups we ride a hundred miles in one day, change horses three or four times during that day and every horse is tired when he's turned loose. An average cowboy's day's riding is over fifty miles, and considering the kind of horses we ride and the country we go over I'm thinking them little flat saddles would be worse than useless.

"Besides we have to have a strong and heavy built saddle for roping. You sure can't hold one of them big wild heavy steers with your little finger after you rope 'em, and sometimes them big steers will drag a horse right along with 'em for a ways after he's caught, and even jerk him down. You see, Scootie, our cattle ain't at all broke to lead, no more than a deer is and it takes a mighty strong horse and rope and saddle to stop and throw 'em. Another thing is, nobody could get on many of our horses with them little flat saddles and if anybody could they couldn't stay on top."

"Yes," says Kip, studying one of the saddles, "I guess you can't fall out of one of these."

"You sure can, if you don't know how to ride. There ain't a saddle made that you can't fall or get throwed out of. If there is and you was to put it on some of our wild horses that bucks pretty good that horse would jar you around so that he'd soon make you wish you could fall off. . . . The saddle ain't what makes a good rider, we

Sometimes them big steers will drag a horse right along with 'em for a ways and even jerk 'em down.

ride by balance more than we do by grip on a bucking horse, and we use no grip on a trotting or running horse no matter how rough the riding is, nothing but balance."

"What do you mean by balance?" asks Kip.

"Well," Uncle Bill's tongue was getting dry, "by balance is where you just sort of feel your horse with one leg and then another without gripping him. You just kind of get the swing of him, figure out which way he's going to go and go with him. That comes natural and with practice in riding, and an average cowboy can follow his horse at full speed over sage brush and rocks with his eyes closed. Many a cowboy has rode asleep on his horse for many a mile. And talk about balance, the next time you go to a rodeo you watch the bare-back bronc riding. That's where cowboys ride hard bucking horses bare back and with nothing to hang onto but a little rope around that horse's middle. He's allowed to use only one hand, too."

"But," says Scootie, getting back to saddles, "it looks to me as if they'd be very uncomfortable to ride."

"I never noticed it, not unless I'm in one for a whole day and a night straight without something to eat, and then my stomach is apt to give me a heap more trouble than my saddle. Of course it's all what a feller is used to, and I'd bet a month's wages that anybody who does the kind of riding we do would soon get to use our kind of saddles and like 'em, no matter what kind of saddles they rode before."

"Why all the leather back of the seat, Uncle Bill?" asks Kip.

"You mean the saddle skirting? Why, sometimes we have to tie things to our saddles and pack 'em a long ways. The skirting protects the horse's back and keeps anything we might tie behind the cantle from digging a sore. The whole saddle is made for use, and protection of the horse, and we think enough of our horses and have to depend on 'em so much to get us wherever we're going or for the work we have to do, that you can bet your boots we don't have anything about our riggings but what's necessary and for the comfort of both horse and rider.

"Like for instance, supposing I was to make a trip and I wanted to take my war-bag along, I might have a box of cartridges or a marlin spike, buckles, hunks of leather and odd things that's got sharp edges. Well, I wouldn't have to ride far before them sharp edges would dig a hole in my horse's back. There's where the saddle skirting does its good work."

"You said something about a war-bag," Kip chips in, "what is a war-bag?"

"A war-bag is a little sack, most always made of canvas where a cowboy throws in all little belongings that would get scattered around and lost. Most anything can be found in one of them little bags, anything from a sweetheart's love letters to a strip of rawhide. There'll be buttons, tobacco, cigarette papers, socks and, well, most anything. We often call them little bagsful our thirty-years'-gathering."

There was many more questions asked about saddles which Uncle Bill done his best to answer. It turned out to be quite a job for him to explain everything they wanted to know so they would understand. He had to do a heap of talking, more than he'd ever done at one time in his life, and he had to go to the spring a couple of times for a drink of water so he could keep up the good work. Them kids could sure ask questions, but the old cowboy didn't mind. Instead he sort of liked it. Their questions was different than any that'd ever been asked of him and many of 'em made him laugh on account they brought up things which he'd never wondered at before, things he was so used to, like part of him, and now the questions made him notice them things for the first time, for them questions was as strange to him as the answers was to the kids.

WILLJAMES
'32

CHAPTER TWO

UNCLE BILL was in the middle of answering a long question when the sounds of hoofs, creaking of saddle leather and jingling of spurs was heard, and Frank and half a dozen riders rode into the corral. The kids popped up in the stable door about then and stared wide-eyed at the riders. They hardly missed any move as the riders begin to get off their horses, and when a couple of the horses started to back-jump and acting up the kids wondered at that and Kip asked:

"What's the matter with them, don't they want the cowboys to get off?"

"It ain't that, they're just spooky, one of 'em is a bronc and the other is just plain ornery and mean."

"What's a bronc, and what makes the other one mean?"

"That's some question you're asking me now, Son. . . . A bronc is an unbroke or part broke horse, and what makes the other one mean is nothing excepting that he's just natural born that way, like some humans. That horse don't want to work. He don't want no saddle nor man on him and his main ambition is to fight to be free. It takes a mighty good man to handle such kind and get any work out of 'em."

17

Uncle Bill was in the middle of answering a long question.

"Oh, look," says Scootie. "That man is sticking his thumb in the horse's eye. What does he do that for?"

"He ain't sticking his thumb in his eye," Uncle Bill laughed, "he's pulling the eyelid down over it so the horse won't see him while he's getting off."

"Why don't he want the horse to see him?"

"He'd strike and kick at him before he could reach the ground, and he can do that plenty fast too."

The kids got a chance to see the horse show his meanness that way, for even tho the cowboy kept the eye closed with his thumb that wise horse could feel the rider slide off and he done his best to reach him with a hind hoof. But the rider was wise too. He had to be or he wouldn't been able to ride him. He didn't jump away from the horse as he slid out of his saddle. Instead of that he hung close and right alongside his shoulder his feet never touching the ground, and when the horse quit kicking and stood for a second he slipped away from him, in a way that made the kids think he had all the time in the world. They was surprised to see a lit cigarette in his mouth, and he looked as cool and unflustrated as tho he'd just stepped out of the bunk house door.

The unsaddling of that horse come next, and as the cowboy reached for a short heavy rope, Kip asked, "What is he going to do, whip him? . . . He deserves it."

"No. It don't do any good to whip a horse like that, it would only make him fight all the more. We do better than whip such kind, we ride 'em."

"He looks as if he ought to get more riding, then, he's so mean and fat."

"Well, we have lots of horses, and that horse won't be rode again for about three days because there's many others that needs as much riding as he does."

While the talk was going on the cowboy went to unsaddling. He flipped one end of the short rope around the horse's front feet to where he could reach that end from a safe distance, then he tied a slip knot, making a loop which he drawed tight around both ankles. From

He didn't jump away from the horse as he slid out of his saddle.

that time on the horse only quivered and not a hoof left the ground as the cowboy went to unsaddling him. He had more fear of that rope binding his front feet together than anything else, for he'd been throwed hard and layed flat to the ground many a time for acting up when his ankles was tied that way. He never forgot that, and the feel of that rope changed him sudden from a fighting wild cat to a quivering statue.

The horses was unsaddled and turned out of the corral into a big pasture, the cowboys grinned at the kids as they started for the cook house and as one of 'em went by he gave them a wink, looked at Uncle Bill and says, "Hello Grandma."

"Drift along you wind-belly."

The kids had to laugh at that and Kip had to ask what a wind-belly was.

"That's what we sometimes call a stunted orphan calf, all belly, fat in the middle and poor at both ends."

"But that man didn't look that way."

The old cowboy couldn't say nothing to that, and Frank came around the stable in time to sort of relieve him for a spell.

"Well," says Frank, "let's all go throw a bait."

Kip and Scootie hopped along after him, but not before they asked what a bait was.

"A bait," he says, "is something to eat and attract wolves to a trap with, but we ain't no wolves and there won't be no trap, so we'll just eat."

Uncle Bill went on to the cook house to eat with the rest of the cowboys.

There's no noon hour's rest with the cowboy, and fifteen minutes from the time they'd went in the cook house they was out again and headed for the corrals. Fresh horses had been brought in, and in a short while there was loops sailing out for the heads of the ones that was wanted.

Kip and Scootie hurried thru their meal as they noticed the dust by the corrals. They didn't want no desert, and they made it in time to come in the big gate before the last horses was caught. They wouldn't of missed watching the roping of 'em for anything, nor the saddling either.

The same cowboy they'd watched unsaddle the mean horse before the noon meal had caught another one of the same kind, and with the help of a gentle saddle horse was dragging him to where his saddle layed.—A cowboy never packs a saddle to a horse, he takes the horse to it.

"Gee, that's a mean horse," says Kip, as he watched him fighting while being led and drug to the saddle. "I wonder what he's going to do with him?"

Scootie couldn't answer that question, but Uncle Bill, who had now seen the kids, came near 'em and answered it. "He's going to ride him," he says, "and give him a little something to do this afternoon."

"Why don't he ride a nice horse?" asked Kip.

"We wouldn't have no nice horses if we didn't ride and gentle 'em. They all act mean at first, and that gentle horse you see your Uncle Frank saddling now, he was just as mean at one time."

Kip and Scootie couldn't quite understand that. From what they'd seen of horses in the streets and parks and read of 'em in books they'd got to know of the horse as being gentle and kind always, and now they couldn't figure out some of these western horses that acted plum against what they'd thought a horse to be.

"What makes 'em be so wild?" asks Scootie.

"Nature," says Uncle Bill. "Every animal is a wild animal by nature, dogs, cats, horses, cattle and all animals. The tame ones you see around homes and farms are tame only because they're raised amongst humans. They've been bred and cross-bred for hundreds of years so as to get the different sizes for the uses that the human wanted of 'em. But with all the upbreeding the wildness is still there, and if us humans was to disappear from the earth for some years and then return, we'd see all our domesticated animals and pets gone back to the wild bunch. The tom cat that sticks by the stove of winters would turn out to be as much wild cat as the wild cat is. Rover, the dog would soon show his wolf instinct and change to be as much wolf as the wolf is. Bossie, the cow would hightail it for the plains and forget what a milk bucket looked like. The horse Prince would kick the stable door open, jump the pasture fence and go to running wild with others of his kind. No feed of grain or lump of sugar would bring him back and he'd have to be roped and tied down before the bridle could be put on his head again."

The kids were watching the cowboy saddle the mean horse as Uncle Bill talked. They was taking in every word he said and beginning to understand, but it was hard for them to believe that such tame animals and pets as they'd seen and knowed would get wild again as the old cowboy said.

Here Uncle Bill came up with some proof. "You see that fighting horse the cowboy is saddling," he went on. "Well, you maybe wouldn't believe that less than a year ago he was as gentle as any horse you ever seen. He'd just been broke and was acting fine, then he got away and run out on the range and when he was run in again this spring he had to be broke all over again. He'll be harder to break this time too because he's wise now and knows how and when to fight. A bronc that's just been broke and then gets away is always harder to break over again then he was the first time. The first time he's only wild and not much else. He's rattled and don't know how to fight his rider, and by the time he gets his senses he's sort of used to the rider and saddle. But if he gets away and gets time to think things over he's sure apt to make use of his first experience with that rider and make him earn his wages. He'll be harder to corral too, and if he gets amongst a bunch of wild ones you'll most

likely see him take the lead when a rider is spotted on
the skyline. He'll be wiser, braver and cooler headed
than the wild ones and make the bunch a good leader."

The action that went on in the corral about then
sort of gave a mighty lively illustration of many things
that Uncle Bill had tried to explain. The mean horse
had turned out to be sure enough mean, and even tho
the cowboy was patient and tried hard to have him stand
while he slipped the saddle on him, he finally had to

*When he was run in
again this spring he had
to be broke all over again.*

throw him, tie him down and saddle him while flat on the ground. The horse being hobbled and with one hind foot tied up, had already throwed himself a couple of times while fighting and it was to save him strength for the ride that was ahead that he was throwed and saddled where he layed.

The saddle cinched tight, the cowboy slipped into it while the horse was down. Another took the foot ropes off and the horse was free to get on his feet. How he got on his feet was a sight for the kids that beat anything they'd ever seen in any circus or show and they sort of shivered for a second. For the horse didn't get on his feet, he just blowed up in the air the same as if he'd been laying on a volcano that busted up sudden. The rider took the jolt, found all of his saddle while he was in middle air and took on a few more jolts up there. All that in the wink of an eye, and when the horse hit the ground, after making a half circle in the air, the earth itself seemed to pop. And something did sure enough pop. The strain that the horse put against the latigo and cinch was too much. The strong latigo broke at the cinch ring, and saddle and rider left the horse together.

The whole outfit had no more than left the horse when he followed it up and bucked right over it. The rider layed close to earth, buried his head by his saddle, while hoofs was everywhere.

How that rider wasn't killed right then was a heap more than the kids could figure out, and they was surprised again when, after the horse bucked away, to see the rider stand up without any loss of tan. Instead he went to rolling a smoke and examining his saddle without a glance at the horse that'd bucked it and him off. It was all in the day's work.

A new latigo was put on the saddle, the horse was roped, throwed and saddled once more, and this time the saddle stuck. So did the rider. It was some ride, for the horse having one victory was sure working for another, and he bucked better than ever.

A horse doesn't breathe while he's bucking, and it was as the horse stopped to take on some air that Kip managed to say:

"Gee, Uncle Bill, that man had better get off before he gets hurt."

The strong latigo broke at the cinch ring and saddle and rider left the horse together.

That remark seemed to hit that old cowboy's funny bone and he had a good laugh before he could get up an answer to it.

"We wouldn't have no gentle horses if we was to get off of 'em every time they acted up," he says, finally. "We'd all be wearing moccasins instead of boots and walking instead of riding."

The horse lit into bucking again soon as the rider started to stir him out of his tracks. It was a fine job of bucking, and even tho the rider was loosened a bit a couple of times he done a fine job of whipping it out of him, for the time being. All was a mighty strange and exciting sight to the kids, and as the corral gate was opened and all the cowboys rode out, that mean horse was the cause of starting a couple more horses to do the same. They'd just sort of been waiting for an excuse.

The kids watched the riders lope away. The mean horse still took spells at his bucking and it wasn't till he was left behind a bit that his bucking went to long crowhops and then a head-fighting lope.

"That man can ride well, can't he, Uncle Bill?" says Scootie, as she watched the riders making distance and stirring a dust. "I can't understand how he managed to stay on that horse at all."

"You bet he can ride, and he's sure got to ride rough string on this outfit."

"Rough string?"

"Yes. A rough string is made up of the meanest horses an outfit has. A special good rider is hired to get some work out of 'em, also the meanness. Sometimes they gentle down some, but when work is over for a spell and they're turned out again that meanness most generally comes back at the first saddling after their rest. Yes, a rough string rider has to be a good rider, even better than the man who just breaks horses, and with that kind of riding he's either all crippled up in a few years or else his body turns out to be all rawhide and spring steel.

"Did you see how the horse stomped all over that rider when he bucked him and saddle off? . . . Well, if it'd been anybody not hardened to that kind of work you'd of heard some bones snap, you can bet on that. I seen a bronc kick a cowboy right in the stomach with both hind feet one time and send him a sailing for about twenty feet, and that cowboy hardly lost a breath. Of course if that horse had got him just right he might of killed him, but I rode the range enough and seen things happen that made even me wonder what a cowboy is made of. I've seen horses turn over in the air and fall on top of 'em, or stampede away thru thick timber and down over rocky ledges, but most always, even tho the clothes was tore and the skin was barked up some, the cowboy would be still all together. Of course some get hurt and mighty bad once in a while. Some get killed and mighty quick, too, but it's sure enough pure accident when that happens. Everything has to gang up against him.

"I'm telling you this so you'll know what kind of man it takes to ride the rough string."

"Did you ever ride the rough string?" asks Scootie.

Uncle Bill didn't know just how to answer that. After what he'd just said he sort of felt that he'd be blowing about himself if he said that he did, but there was no way out of that for he sure enough had rode the rough string, and for many years. He finally managed to say that he had and he looked like he wanted to apologize as he said it.

There was more such questions asked about himself which he didn't at all care to answer, and when they got to coming too fast he walked over to his saddle with the excuse that he had to ride away to look over some stock somewhere in the hills. But if that excuse changed the subject sudden, the kids sure didn't mind the change. They hopped right after him, and both with eyes a-sparkling asked him if they could go too.

Uncle Bill hadn't thought about their wanting to go. He wasn't used to youngsters and didn't as yet know that they're always up and rearing to go when something new and exciting pops up. Riding was one of them things, and as the old cowboy turned to look at Kip and Scootie, so all anxious and smiling, he found that it would of been just about as hard to say no as hitting a new born colt with a club. He'd had no intentions of riding away. He'd just said that as an excuse to change the line of questions they'd been asking him. But now it looked like he was in for it, and all he could do was grin at their expressions and say:

"Yes, I guess so." He looked over the horses that'd been left in the corral, and went on, "But I'll have to go in the pasture and run in some horses that you two can ride. There's none here that'd do."

"Don't bring me an old plug, will you Uncle Bill?" says Kip. "I want a horse that can go fast, one that's full of pep."

Uncle Bill had to grin some more at that. "Did you ever ride before?" he asks.

Kip grinned, too. "Yes," he says, "on a Merry-go-around."

"I'll get you both a good horse, but you better go to the house till I get back. I won't be gone long."

From their first hour at the ranch the kids was dressed with clothes fitting to their vacation there. Both Kip and Scootie wore overalls, boots and big hats which had been bought before they left the city. They'd already wore them outfits before leaving home and had been anxious to try them out. Now they was at last going to have a chance, and as they walked up to the house they kept looking back to see which way the old cowboy was riding. They didn't go into the house, just stayed on the porch and watched, and when Martha came out and asked them if they'd like their desert now they still didn't have much appetite for such, for the first time in their lives. But being they had a spell to wait they finally agreed that they would take their desert.

It seemed a long time before they seen Uncle Bill returning with a bunch of horses and they was down to the corrals quite a while before he got there. They watched him bringing the horses in at a walk and Kip says to Scootie. "I thought he was going to *run* 'em in. He said so."

There was quite a few unbroke and snorty horses in the bunch, and on account of the kids being in sight there was some trouble in corralling the bunch. A few of the broncs broke back and finally Uncle Bill had to

". . . but they're sure scared of them too."

tell the kids to get in the stable and keep out of sight. But they came out again, skipping and a-hopping, soon as the horses was corralled and the gate was closed. The broncs had such a fit at the sight of 'em that they jammed one another against the corral pretty hard, and the old cowboy had to speak to 'em some more.

"Better keep away. These horses ain't used to seeing anybody jumping around so close, and if you crowd 'em too much one of 'em might get excited, break out of the bunch and run over the top of you."

The kids kept away but it was mighty hard for them to do that. They wanted to look the horses over at close range and pick out the ones they was going to ride, pretty ones. But the pretty ones was most all wild and unbroke and they'd sure never do.

"What makes them look prettier than the broke horses," says Uncle Bill, "is because they're up on their toes, heads up, always watching and ready to jump in case anything strange, us for instance, comes near 'em. And, the same as any wild animal. They're more scared and suspicious of a human than anything else on earth."

"I read in a book once," says Scootie, "that we look ten times as big to a horse as we really are, and maybe that's why these are scared of us."

"I heard of that too, but I sure don't think it's true, not according as to how well they can judge their distance when they strike or kick at a cowboy when he comes near a mean one."

"But why are they so scared of us? They're so much stronger and bigger than we are."

"That's beyond me, unless it's their natural instinct that keeps a warning 'em. A mountain lion is not so big and a rattle snake is mighty little as compared to a horse but they're sure scared of them too."

"But we don't harm them like a lion or a snake would."

"Well, anyhow, they sure act like we're all poison and claws just the same, and when a rider catches an unbroke horse and puts his hand on his neck for the first time that horse flinches just the same as tho there were fangs on the fingers of that hand. It takes mighty strong ropes to hold him."

CHAPTER THREE

THE SUBJECT OF THE HORSE and his enemies came to stop as Uncle Bill took his rope down off his saddle and made a loop. He caught one gentle horse and then another and both of 'em was soon saddled and bridled, the kids watching every move the old cowboy made.

"These horses are pretty good size for you kids," he says, "but that won't matter once you learn how to get on 'em, and that's what I'm going to start teaching you now."

He took the bridle reins of one of the horses. "First," he went on, "you got to have control of your horse's head and you got to remember that the reins is what you hold and steer him with. I seen a tenderfoot get excited one time when his horse started to run. He dropped his reins, hollered "whoa" and grabbed the saddle horn. He'd of been going yet I guess if I hadn't caught his horse. Our horses are not broke to know what "whoa" or "giddap" means. A little pull on the reins stops 'em and a touch of the spur starts 'em. But I'm not going to let you have no spurs to day, not till you learn how to ride a bit and what spurs are for. You can just touch 'em with your bare boot heels and that'll do pretty near as good."

Drawing the bridle reins over the horse's neck he took a mane holt along with the reins with his left hand. "Now," he says, "never draw your reins too tight because that's apt to make the horse fret and move around. Draw 'em just tight enough so there won't be too much slack in 'em and so you'll have control of his head. Then you reach for your stirrup like this with your right hand and stick your left foot in it, but not all the way in to the heel, just about halfways so that in case the horse jerks away from you before getting in the saddle you won't be running no danger of getting it caught in the stirrup and being drug around. Many 'bronc twisters' (horse breakers) never touch a stirrup with their hands. They reach for it with their boot toe and while standing close to the horse's shoulder, but it takes practice to do that and do it well.

"Now, after you get your foot in the stirrup you reach up for the saddle horn, give yourself a little boost and get in the saddle as easy and smooth as you can without using too much time. It takes a heap of practice to get on a horse well, and seldom does anybody learn how while riding only gentle horses because, with gentle horses, a rider is not careful. There's plenty of time and it's all the same if that rider just flops in the saddle like a soggy sack of potatoes. But you sure can't get on a mean horse that way. There's where you got to use everything you got in you, not in main strength and awkwardness but by smooth and easy balance of yourself.

"I can always tell a good rider and a man that's rode mean horses by the way he gets on one. He's got the grace and smoothness of a panther and it don't seem to be no effort at all to him to slide up in the saddle. That's on account of perfect control of every muscle and which can be got only thru years of experience in riding mean horses. It's more important to be able to get on a horse well than it is to be able to stay after you get on top of him. For you're sure out of luck if you get off your horse somewhere out in the hills and can't get back on him, and fact is you're not a real good rider unless you can do that well, and mighty well, on any kind of wild or tame horse. Nobody ever holds a horse for a cowboy to get on while out on the range, and many are slippery as an eel and quick as lightning in their trying to get away from him.

"Sometime, after you two get on to riding some I'll have you practice getting on and off a horse without the saddle being cinched. That's not so easy to do with a horse that's got low withers and the worst that can happen to you is have the saddle slide off before you get in it. And getting on a horse without the saddle being cinched will make you use every muscle you have in the right way, not in an awkward way and like as tho you was just dead weight trying to get up there.

"In getting on a horse the rider pretty well controls his whole body with his right arm. With a hold of the saddle horn he manouvers his actions according to the actions of the horse, and there's where practicing getting on a horse without the saddle being cinched helps some. Of course you could be able to do that and not be able at all to get on a mean horse but it'll sure take the awkwardness out of you in being able to get on a gentle one.

"I seen some cowboys using the cantle instead of the saddle horn to help themselves up on a horse with, but them was mostly old fellers and riding gentle horses. I never seen a bronc twister getting on a mean horse do that. And here's a good stunt you want to practice sometime, try and get on a horse while holding both hands in the air and without touching the saddle with either of 'em. Of course that's just a stunt and not to be tried on a mean horse, but if you get to be able to do that it'll sure make you come to time in learning how to use your balance and how to get on a horse well."

While talking, the old cowboy went thru the different actions and got on and off his horse many times. He done mighty fine till he come to that stunt he just spoke of, and he would of backed out in showing 'em how it was done but neither Kip or Scootie would let him, they wanted to see it done. That sort of teached Uncle Bill a lesson as a teacher, not to try and teach anything he couldn't do himself.

"I'm not so good at them tricks any more," he says. "Too old and stiff, besides I ain't done that for more than twenty years."

But he couldn't dissappoint the kids, and after the third try he made it, but not too well.

"You see," he says, sort of apologizing. "My left leg has only been broke three times and I can't depend on it like I used to."

Try and get on a horse while holding both hands in the air.

39

The kids was now anxious to try their hand at getting on a horse, and they wanted to learn by action what all had been explained to 'em. Uncle Bill was ready to quit talking too. He'd already surprised himself as to how long winded he was, and now he figured he could rest a bit and just watch the kids. But he'd figured wrong and, the kids, even tho they thought they understood pretty well got all mixed up soon as they took holt of the bridle reins. Kip even made the mistake of sticking his right foot in the stirrup instead of the left and it took him quite a while to figure out why he couldn't get in the saddle.

"That ain't a wagon you're getting up into there, Son," says Uncle Bill, laughing. "If you want to use that foot to get on your horse with you'll have to get on the other side of him, the Indian side, and I wouldn't advise trying that only on an Indian-broke horse."

Uncle Bill had to keep on talking and coaching, telling and showing them how to do this and that over and over again. He spent near an hour teaching 'em how to get on and off their horses, but by the time he got thru with that first lesson he felt that he'd given 'em a good start, and with plenty of practice they'd soon be good at that. It was a great help to him that the kids was smart and so anxious to learn, and as Kip had already remarked, he was sure going to be a cowboy some day.

"Well, this is one of the million things you'll have to learn to be a good one," Uncle Bill had said.

Starting, turning and stopping a horse came next in the teaching and he proceeded to coach 'em on that. "As we ride along," he says, "you can sort of watch how I handle my bridle reins, that'll teach you about as much as I can tell you."

Most every western horse starts the second a rider sticks his foot in the stirrup, but the two gentle old ponies that'd been caught for the kids stood stock still. They knowed as well as the old cowboy that their riders was just beginners and they was past the stage of taking advantage of that.

"Now," says Uncle Bill, after him and the kids was in their saddles and ready, "hold both reins in your left hand and give 'em some slack, then just touch your horse's sides with your heels and here we go." He kept on talking as the ponies started. "In case you're riding after cattle and want your horse to start or go fast all you got to do is hit your horse with your heels a little

Kip had already remarked he was sure going to be a cowboy some day.

41

harder. That all depends if you're riding a lazy or lively horse. On a lively horse you have to hold a tighter rein and if you want him to go faster you just give the reins some slack and you don't have to touch him with neither heels nor spurs."

They rode out of the corral and straight ahead for a ways, and then the old cowboy proceeded to educate the kids in how to neckrein, turn, and stop a horse. "First," he says, "and to get the best work out of your horse, you got to find out what kind of a mouth he's got,—wether it's a tender mouth, a good mouth, or a hard mouth. Tender mouthed horses are dangerous for anybody that don't know how to ride. I don't know why it is but most green riders will start pulling on the reins soon as a tender mouthed horse starts to back up. The horse is backing up only to relieve the pull of the bit on his mouth and maybe the green rider is just excited when he pulls all the more. Anyway, and while I was in the army during the war I seen many green riders pull tender mouthed horses over backwards and right on top of 'em by not knowing enough to give their reins some slack.

"Of course there's mean horses that'll fall over backwards no matter what you do, and the safest medecine I found for that was to give the reins some slack soon as I felt it coming and slam my left paw on their knowledge bump between their ears. Most any horse will put his head down soon as he feels it there, and

*You've got your hand in a good place to shove yourself away
in case the horse keeps coming over backwards.*

if he don't you've got your hand in a good place to shove yourself away in case he keeps a-coming over backwards. If you've had enough experience at that you'll land on your feet and the horse's head will land right near 'em. You'll still have a hold of your reins, too."

Being Uncle Bill was now started on the subject he kept on talking and hardly paid any attention to how the kids was riding or if they was listening to what he said. Of course they listened some, but the thrill of their first ride didn't leave much room for their interest but just that. They hadn't even asked any questions for a long time.

"Getting back to horses' mouths," Uncle Bill went on, "an average cowboy can tell what kind of mouth a horse has got the minute he puts a bridle on him and he'll work him according. If he's got a tender mouth he'll use what we call a 'light hand' and for a hard mouth he'll use a 'heavy hand,' which means light or hard pulls. The rider who can do that well can get the best work that any horse might have in him and use the same bit on all kinds. You don't have to have a severe bit to handle a horse. If anything a severe bit aggravates 'em and makes 'em worse and, myself, I wouldn't have nothing but a light curb bit like I got on my bridle now and I'd never use a shank that's more than three inches long from the mouth-piece."

A light curb bit.

The kids was going to ask what a shank and mouth-piece was, but a look at the bit seemed all that was necessary for the time being. They'd remember what it looked like, and if they ever bought one it'd be of the same kind.

Uncle Bill rode silent for a spell and then, of a sudden, he stopped his horse. The two old cowponies, being wise to range riders ways, stopped too, just as sudden, and stock still. The kids wasn't looking for anything like that and kept on a-going till they got to the saddle horn where they come to a mighty surprised stop. They both got quite a thrill at their loss of balance and the old cowboy had a hard time to keep from laughing as he noticed the expression on their faces while they leaned over their horses' necks and hung on to their manes. He turned his head and let on that he hadn't seen 'em and, while laughing to himself, he figured that one good lesson in the kids developing a sense of balance and learning to set on a horse right instead of like a pack as they had.

"Well, now, Kids," he says, "I'm going to try and show you how to handle your bridle reins and how to neckrein a horse, but first I'm going to show you how to hold 'em and that's not at all the way you're holding yours, Scootie," he says to the girl. Scootie had the ends of her reins all tangled up in and around her hands.

Uncle Bill went on: "You hold your reins together between the second and third finger of your left hand and let the ends hang down on the left side of you. You'll find out why that is as you learn more about

You'll need both hands doing that and you can't let your reins go.

riding,—when you want to use both of your hands for some reason or other and still have holt of your reins, like shooting a rifle for instance, or throwing a rope. You'll need both of your hands doing that, and you sure can't let your reins go. Now don't forget, Scootie, and don't ever ball up your reins like you had 'em a while ago. Your horse might fall, get on his feet before you do and drag you around a considerable if them reins got tangled up around your waist.

"We're going to put our horses into a trot pretty soon," Uncle Bill went on, "and while trotting you hold your reins a little tighter than you do while walking your horse, and tighter yet when you put him in a lope. The faster you travel the tighter you hold your reins, as tight as your horse's mouth will let you, because a tight rein steadies him while he's traveling fast. He'll be less apt to fall and if he stumbles and does start to fall you have a chance to pull his head up and keep him from it."

Here one of the kids finally came up with a question. It was Kip.

"Does a horse fall often?" he asks.

"Not a good one. I haven't had a horse fall with me for about a year and I've done a heap of riding in that time. Of course I been riding good and gentle horses, the same as you kids are riding now. Just hold your reins the way I told you and you won't have no trouble at all."

The kids was very careful to hold their reins like they'd been told as Uncle Bill started his horse. Their horses started of their own accord and the three was on their way some more.

"Let's stir 'em into a trot now," says the old cowboy. "Draw your reins a little tighter and touch 'em with your heels, put more weight in your stirrups and grip with your knees just a little bit if you want to for a starter, but I never do. And don't try to sit tight in your saddle, just straight up and ride on balance all you can."

The horses was stirred into a trot and the kids went to reaching for a holt of the saddle horn right away. Uncle Bill come near telling 'em to leave loose and ride straight but he thought he'd better not this first time. He'd do that some other time and after they got their bearings and more used to riding. Many a good cowboy leans over and rests his hands on his saddle or horse's neck while at a trot. That's to sort of ease the jolts and it's sometimes a habit. Many a good cowboy will also lean ahead and grab a holt of his horse's mane but that's either to help his horse while going up a steep hill or steady a tender mouthed one when the reins can't be pulled on, and not at all to hang on. The kids was giggling as they bobbed all over their saddles at the start of the trotting pace. They bounced up and came down hard at every step their horses took. Kip laughed and Scootie squealed and the old cowboy watching 'em had to laugh too.

"Stay with it, Kids," he says, sort of encouraging 'em, "you'll soon get onto it and the first thing you know you'll be settling down to good riding, if you do enough of it."

The trotting pace was kept up for a couple of miles acrost level country and then was slowed down to a walk again, and to another sudden stop. The kids done better that time and didn't get off balance so much.

"We been riding straight ahead," says Uncle Bill, as the kids settled down in their saddles, "but now we're going to wind around in the hills some, and before we do that I want you two to learn how to neckrein and turn your horses. With race horses and such like, the rider uses one hand on each rein and each one of them reins are pulled separate. But being that quick turning horses is more necessary to us out here and that we got to use both hands for other work besides handling our reins, we break our horses to neckrein, which means that we guide our horses with only three fingers of our left hand, like this."

Here he rode ahead a few yards and proceeded to show them what he meant. He turned his horse this way and that way and every way that a horse can be turned, slow and easy at first so the kids could watch, and then faster and quicker so they could get the action of both horse and rider along with the handling of the reins. Before long the old cowboy had his horse at full speed. Then he'd pivot him on his hind legs of a sudden and, as the old saying goes amongst the cowboys, "turn him on a dime," and quicker than the eye could follow. In some turns the horse leaned over so that the rider's foot near touched the ground.

The kids watched the actions of horse and rider with a heap more than plain interest, but they was dubious as to ever being able to do what old Uncle Bill was doing right then. He slowed his horse down again, and riding back and forth and turning his horse in front of 'em he went on to explain the ways of neckreining.

"About the easiest way to learn that," he says, "is to remember to keep both reins in one hand and at even length from the bit. Then all you have to do if you want to turn your horse to any direction is just sort of point the hand that holds the reins towards that direction and the feel of the rein on the horse's neck will make him turn that way, that is if your horse is broke to neckrein like our horses are out here. Sometimes you might have to point past the direction you want to go so as your horse will get to feel the rein enough to turn, that all depends on how well your horse is broke to neckrein.

"Let's ride on now and see what you two can do.

They done pretty well for beginners, and before they come to a point amongst the foothills where Uncle Bill thought they'd all better turn back for the ranch they had a fair idea in the ways of neckreining a horse.

"No use riding too far the first day," says the old cowboy. "You'd only get sore and stiff. It's best to harden in slow and gradual."

"But I'm not a bit tired," says Scootie.

"Me either," Kip chips in.

"Sure not, but you'll feel that you been riding by

the time tomorrow comes and, what's more, we won't be back any too soon for supper. Martha will be looking for you and she told me to be sure and always bring you back in time for your meals. So, if you want to amble on now and travel a little faster go ahead and play tatoo on your ponies' ribs. The faster you want to go the more tatoo you'll have to play."

The kids started their horses into a trot. There was some more giggling and bouncing. The ponies was traveling better now, they was headed towards home, where they'd be unsaddled and turned loose again. A tighter rein had to be held on 'em.

But if the kids bounced high and hit the saddle hard they wasn't a bit scared, and Kip surprised Uncle Bill by asking him if it was alright to let his horse go faster. Scootie seemed to be for more speed too.

It was a wonder to the old cowboy that they stayed on as it was and without going faster. He didn't want 'em to go any faster, but he finally thought it best not to let 'em know that on account it might shake their confidence and make 'em a little scared. A scared rider never is a good one and is more likely to get hurt.

Nobody knowed that better than Uncle Bill did. "Sure it's alright," he says. "I'll be right along with you."

CHAPTER FOUR

HEADED TOWARDS HOME the ponies showed more life. All the kids had to do was to touch 'em with their heels a couple of times and they went faster, the kids also bounced higher and their giggling turned to squealing and hollering. But they was due for more thrill, for, as the ponies was trotting as fast as they could and Kip and Scootie touched 'em once more with their heels, they of a sudden broke into a faster gait, and bounced 'em into a long lope.

The change of gait come near taking the breath away from 'em for a second. They bounced higher than ever and used both hands in grabbing everything they could get a hold of, but they hardly stopped laughing, only during the sudden change of gaits, and even tho they bounced higher now the bounces was easier and further apart than when trotting.

Watching 'em close, the old cowboy was afraid for a spell that they might fall off, and he didn't laugh like they did. But he didn't need to worry none. Not with the grip they had on both saddle horn and mane.

"Be sure and hang on to your reins too," he says, keeping close to them, "and don't drop 'em, because

They bounced higher than ever and used both hands in grabbing everything they could get a hold of.

they're your steering wheel when you're on a horse, and your brake, too."

They hung on to their reins, and everything else they already had, and as the pace was kept up they gradually got used to it enough so they even dared look to one side and shoot a grinning glance at Uncle Bill once in a while.

At the pace they was going it didn't take long to cover the few miles back to the ranch. The horses was getting sweated up, and before they come to the last mile Uncle Bill told the kids to slow down. He could of stopped his horse sudden as he'd already done while trotting, and the kids' horses would of stopped sudden too. But that didn't come to his mind while going at the faster gait because the kids would be sure to fall off.

All slowed their horses down to a trot and then to a walk again. "The reason you should always slow down if your horse is sweated up," says the old cowboy, "is so that he'll have a chance to cool and dry gradual before you turn him loose. That ain't so important in the summer time, if you keep him from taking a drink of cold water right away. But in the winter time if you turn your horse loose while he's warm and sweaty he's mighty apt to catch a bad cold, like any human, and die."

The horses was good and dry by the time they got to the corrals, and as the kids got down to the ground again they got the queer feeling that everybody gets after their first ride. It was like as tho they'd shrunk to half their size all of a sudden, and when they started to walk they felt that their legs was still around a horse. They looked at one another and begin to laugh and, Uncle Bill hearing 'em, turned and wondered what they was laughing at. For he'd long ago forgot what that feeling was like.

"Well, Kids," he says, after the laughing spell was over some, "take care of your horses now, a good cowboy always does that. Unsaddle 'em and put your saddles and bridles away, and then take your horses to the creek and wash their backs. That keeps 'em from getting galded."

They was glad to do all of that, and with Uncle Bill's coaching, it was more learning as to how to really know a horse and the rigging that was used on him. They watched the old cowboy and done as he did, but when the horses was turned loose and rolled in the dirt neither of the kids seen any use in washing their backs, and they had their say about it.

Uncle Bill listened and then grinned. "Yep," he says. "It sure don't look like there's much use, but that's clean dirt they're rolling on now and not like that sweaty dirt we washed off. The next time we ride 'em we'll brush their backs before saddling 'em, and that way we'll never make a sore.

"You got to be good to your horses," he went on, "because they're going to give you a lot of fun and get you where you can see and do a lot of things, if you treat 'em right. Besides that they're going to be your teachers and learn you more about riding in one day than I can by talking a whole month. All a man can do is coach you at the start, how to bridle and saddle your horse, how to get on him and handle your reins. After that's done the man is about thru and the horse comes in as the teacher. He'll be a good one too, and, as the old saying goes, that 'practice makes perfect,' it also goes with riding, and the more you ride, and the more you ride different horses along with your learning the quicker you'll learn. Every horse is different in gait and action and disposition, and the variety along with plenty of riding is what makes you a rider, not talk."

"Do you think I'll ever be as good a rider as you, Uncle Bill?" asks Kip.

"I sure don't see why not. You might be better than me even before the summer is over, that all depends on you."

The old cowboy was mighty modest to say that last. But to see how happy them words made Kip sure was worth while. There was only one distant cloud for that boy right then and that was the thought of the city again when fall come.

"But what about girls, Uncle Bill?" Scootie asks. "Can we get to be as good riders as the boys, and can a girl work on a ranch, and do you think I'll ever be as good a rider as you, and . . ."

"Hold on there, Scootie. Run them questions by one at a time. . . . I'm thinking," he went on, "that *he* riders are the only ones that can get a job on a ranch, unless it's a cooking job. The cowboy's work is all man's work and none for the fair sex to try and do if they want to stay fair. But don't feel bad about that, Scootie, and don't worry about getting to be as good a rider as me because you'll be able to do that easy. There's a little girl living the other side of the mountain who is about as handy on a horse as anybody would want to be. Her dad has a nice size herd and her and him handled it alone, all excepting at branding time. She's mighty good with a rope too.

"Yes, I know of quite a few girls on different ranches who are mighty good hands and a great help to their pappies. Then I know of widow ladies who manage some pretty big outfits and, thru the experience of their late husbands, do a mighty good job at it.

"So you don't have to worry, Scootie, and, anyhow, in a few years more you'll meet some nice young feller in the city that'll make you forget all about horses and ranches, and this old decrepit cowboy who coached you on your first ride."

Scootie had an answer ready to go against that last remark, but it was stopped short by a sort of yodle call from the house. It was Martha calling the kids to supper.

"Run along now," says Uncle Bill, "and take your time eating. Your uncle and the other riders won't be back for an hour or so yet and it'll still be plenty light for you two to come back down and watch 'em unsaddle."

They took their time, as the old cowboy told 'em to, but they figured he must of misjudged some because they was no more than thru eating their last hunk of pie when they looked down to the corrals and seen the riders had come and was beginning to unsaddle. They chewed their last bite on the way down from the house and reached the corrals just in time to see the cowboy with the mean horse in action.

The mean horse had been worked all right. That could be seen from the dry sweat on him, but he didn't seem tired and he went to acting up again as the cowboy started to get off of him. The thumb done the work of pulling the eyelid down over one eye, and the same smooth action of that rider was brought on again as he eased himself out of the saddle, slid down along the horse's shoulder and away from him. A striking front hoof came up as the lid was let go and there wasn't many inches between it and the rider. Soon a loop spread and brought both the horse's front feet together. The horse was tired but he fought till he finally throwed himself. He was unsaddled the same way as he'd been saddled, flat to the ground. And even tho he was ready to fight some more and till a last breath stopped him, a half a day's work was got out of him just the same.

The horses all unsaddled and turned out, Uncle Frank came near the kids and, with a wide grin, asked 'em what kind of time they had during the day.

"Oh, fine," they both said at once. "And Uncle Bill

told me," Kip went on, "that I might be as good a rider as he is before the summer is over."

"Me too," says Scootie.

Uncle Frank winked at the old cowboy. "That ought to be easy enough," he says, "if you do as he tells you, along with plenty of riding."

The kids didn't follow their Uncle Frank up to the house, they sort of hinted that they'd like to be with the cowboys around the bunk house and it was agreed that they could visit there for a spell. The bunk house was a long low log building with a red dirt roof that

The bunk house was a long low log building with a red dirt roof that spread over an open space to another of the same kind

spread over an open space to another of the same kind that was the cook house, where the cook made a hand of himself with pots and pans and grub. The bunk house had drawed many a curious look from the kids on their way back and forth from the corrals, but there'd been so much to do and see that they hadn't a chance to investigate the inside.

Now they had a chance, and while Uncle Bill and the other riders was in the cook house taking on their evening meal, they sniffed everywhere, the same as two cayote pups around a deserted camp. The double row of bunks along the walls was a sight mighty new and strange to 'em. They counted twenty bunks and then went to feeling and looking over everything that hung along 'em. There was "shaps" (leather and hair leggings), pieces of bridles, different kinds of spurs and bits, new and old hats and boots, rifles and six-shooters, clothes and everything that goes to make up a cowboy's belongings. Along with the bedding, which every cowboy owns, none had more than a pack horse could easy carry, and any of 'em could of moved on with all they owned and be fifty miles away in a day's time.

Few cowboys are tied down with belongings, for most of their belongings are "on the hoof" and most cowboys usually have three or four head of horses of their own which they call "privates" and are not used while they're riding for an outfit. When a cowboy goes to work for an outfit he turns his private horses loose on the range or in a pasture and rides the horses that that outfit furnishes him. All he has to furnish is his saddle and roll of bedding, and experience.

Mostly experience, and it's about impossible for a greenhorn to get a job on a regular cow or horse outfit. If one does it'll be as a "flunky" (cook's helper) and working around camp, and if he wants to work up as a cowboy he'll have a chance to ride in his spare time and gradually break into the game. From then on it's all up to his natural ability, staying quality, and nerve as to wether he'll ever be a cowboy or not. Most greenhorns go back to where they come from without getting very far. They find the life pretty rough and soon as the newness wears off they find that reading about the life is more interesting and easier than living it, and then begin to hanker for the home fires and the soft beds they're so used to.

Most cowboys are the sons of cowmen. They're brought up in the saddle, riding and roping and handling range stock from the time they're big enough to walk. They don't know much of anything else and not many care to, for their pride and spirit in being good at the game sort of blots out any other ambition. A few branch out in some other game now and again but half of them will come back to the range. Some that don't, often wish they could, and only responsibility holds 'em where they are.

There's some men brought up on the range that's more fitted for the city and who make good there, the same as there's some men brought up in the city that are more fitted for the range and make good in the cattle game. But not many tenderfeet will stick it out long enough to learn the game. The most of 'em find there's a heap more to learn than they ever figured and being they know of other and easier ways of living they soon go back to that.

The kids was still prowling around the bunk house when there was a jingling of spur rowels and the cowboys begin filing in. After a day's work they was in the habit of stretching out on their bunks and reading from the saddle catalogs, old books and magazines that was on the long table in the center of the floor. Some talked and swapped stories and the lamps didn't burn long after dark come, for daybreak comes mighty early during summer days, and daybreak marks the time for the cowboy to start work.

But at the sight of the kids none of the riders stretched out on their bunks that evening. They just set on the edge of 'em and begin to enjoy the strange and scarce company of the youngsters. Uncle Bill came in, and after some time of quiet and cigarette rolling, one of the riders nicknamed Joker on account of his being talkative, always telling jokes and stories of the kind where truth was a stranger, started the talk going by asking Kip in his usual joking way if he was going to be up in time to help him corral and milk a few antelope before breakfast and gather the eggs from the jack rabbits' nests.

Kip remembered reading once that an antelope was the fastest animal on four feet, and learned long ago that bunnies didn't lay eggs. He didn't answer. Instead he just grinned at the cowboy, then glanced at Uncle Bill, who winked at him and which went as much as to say not to pay no attention.

So Kip didn't answer, but Scootie, who hadn't seen the old cowboy's wink, answered for him and said that her and Kip would be glad to go and help. She had her doubts about corralling antelope and finding jack rabbit eggs, but she didn't worry about that at the thought of being out and riding.

"All right," says Joker, keeping serious, "when you hear the clock strike three I'll be in the corral waiting for you."

WILL JAMES
'30

CHAPTER FIVE

UNCLE FRANK WALKED IN the bunk house as Joker was getting well strung out with some of his pet stories. It wasn't often that Frank spent an evening with his riders, because at that time he was usually busy marking down how many calves might have been branded that day, how many cattle had been gathered, their ages and sexes and what part of the range they'd been shoved to.

So, with Frank and the two kids for company, that evening turned out to be mighty special. Joker dug up a few more of his best jokes, Uncle Bill told a few himself which had more truth and was around range happenings. That all was mighty interesting to the kids. The stories was as strange as the way they was told and even tho there was some parts they didn't understand they listened with all ears. As a rule the cowboy is mighty good at telling stories, and that's because telling stories and jokes and singing are about the only entertainment there is after the day's work is done. The most of 'em have a natural wit and they develop a knack of shaping a story so that most of 'em are made mighty interesting.

Telling jokes and singing are about the only entertainment there is after the day's work is done.

"Did you fellers ever hear of little Sammy Doyle?" asks one of the riders, as the stories slowed down a bit. Nobody had, so he went on to tell about him. "This is true," he says. "Me and a few other cowboys was at the happening and Sammy could prove it if he wanted to. Well, Sammy is a black eyed and hook nosed little feller. I don't think he weighs over a hundred pounds and I know he don't stand more than five feet in his bare heels. When this story begins he's at the home ranch of a horse outfit in Wyoming. There's a big black man cooking for the spread and this fella and Sammy don't get along very well from the start, maybe it's on account that Sammy is little and this feller thinks he can buffalo him.

"But little Sammy don't buffalo worth a doggone and that sort of aggravates the cook, specially when he's sort of proud of having the reputation of being a mighty tough hombre. It was scattered around that he'd killed a couple of men down the Border country and he'd most likely been convicted if it hadn't been for his brother, who went in debt up to his neck and got the best lawyer in the state to save him.

"That didn't cure him none, instead he got to thinking that he sure enough was tough and he stirred up trouble most everywhere he went. He got so he expected everybody to get out of his way, and when Sammy don't budge at all he goes to try and bluff him. The bluffs got to be serious more and more each time and that big cook just sort of camps on Sammy's trail to make trouble.

One time, because Sammy wouldn't be bluffed, he throws an iron picket pin at him, Sammy dodges it, picks it up and sends it right back at him.

"Things go on that way for a spell and Sammy, being of the kind that never looks for trouble, sort of gets tired of having trouble forced on him. He was quiet and peaceful one day and with no interest only to keep his plate filled after coming in from a long ride when the cook gets rambunctious and passes a remark about Sammy that Sammy don't like at all and he splatters a cup of hot coffee on that cook's face. Of course that'd make anybody sort of peeved, and the cook don't get peeved at all, he just gets delirious that way and hunts up a butcher knife. It looks like there's going to be a massacree sure enough, and there is. Sammy don't like the looks of knives much, so, when that big pot wrassler comes his way a frothing at the mouth he knows mighty well that he ain't got no chance close-fighting that big feller, specially when he comes with a knife. Sammy don't know how to run, he'd never learned that trick, and as the cook comes on he about clears the table throwing everything at him that he can get his hands on and trying to stop him. There's potsful of beans and meat a-sailing in the air and lighting on the fella's head, but the pots just dent and bounce off. The cook looks like a walking mulligan stew and he keeps on a-coming.

"Seeing there's no stopping him by throwing hard things at his head, Sammy squares off, levels his six-shooter at him and hollers for him to stop. But wether the cook is too mad to see and reason or thinks that Sammy won't shoot he comes on just the same, and it ain't till the long knife just about grazes Sammy's hide when he pulls the trigger and plugs him right in the birthmark. When the smoke of the forty-five clears there's one man less in the state of Wyoming.

"Sammy replaces the empty cartridge in his six-shooter, and he's putting it back in the holster when the superintendent of the outfit walks in, looks at the dead cook and then at the messed up cook house. He can tell at a glance how everything happened and he don't ask no questions. After a while he tells Sammy that he better ride to town and send out another cook.

"It's night-time by the time Sammy gets in town, locates a cook and lets him have his horse and rigging to get to the ranch on. Then he goes to the sheriff's office and gives himself up.

"The sheriff knows men well, specially men of the range, and after he listens to Sammy he figures it's plain case of self-defense. He puts him in jail till time come for a hearing, and being he's the only one in it at that time the sheriff don't bother getting a keeper to handle the keys. He just gets a promise from Sammy that he won't try to get away and leaves the jail door unlocked.

"All is well that way for a few days. Sammy gets his meals at the Elite Chop House at the county's expense, takes in the town during the day and uses the jail for his hotel when night comes. That was the understanding between him and the sheriff.

"Then one morning the sheriff had to hit out. A bunch of bad fellers are stirring a commotion in one corner of his well-behaved county and them's what he's after, they're his favorite meat. He puts the constable in charge and then's when things sort of changes for Sammy. That constable is all for rules and regulation, besides having a hankering to fill the sheriff's boots in the office. So, while the sheriff is away he scatters around town how the rules of the laws has been neglected, how a killer has been allowed to mingle with the good folks of the fair city, and so on. Sammy gets to hear of that thru some friends who comes to see him. He can't get out to see them no more, for the sheriff has no more than left when the constable locks him up, and from then on his meals are brought to him and sneaked in thru the bars like he was a wildcat.

"Sammy is willing to take his medecine and has nothing against the constable for going according to rules and locking him up, but he sure sees red when he hears how that feller is talking about him and the sheriff around town. He don't care so much what's said about himself, what's said about the sheriff is what gets him in the raw, and he sets his mind to squaring things.

"It's one evening after supper is over, Sammy has filled himself up all he can and it's as the constable comes to get the empty dishes when he sees that a plate that's handed him thru the bars has a gun barrel alongside of it, and pointing straight at his gizard. He don't take that plate. Instead he does as Sammy tells him and unlocks the cell door. Sammy then hits out of the jail and to where a rider is holding a horse for him, the same rider who'd smuggled the gun in.

"That's how come that a day or so later the constable is found locked up in the jail and all by himself. His wife had missed him, nobody else had, and when the news of the escape gets around town the folks got to grinning and remarking how queer it is that the sheriff can keep a prisoner with just a word and the constable can't, not even with locked steel.

"Well, Sammy ain't been seen nor heard of for quite a few months. He's drifted south a thousand miles or so and he's careful not to show himself any more than he can help because he figures that even tho he gets clear in smoking up the cook he would get convicted on jail breaking. He feels he's sort of evened scores by showing up the constable and getting away while that feller had charge. Then one day a northern boy he knows drifts in at the outfit where he's riding and tells him how the constable is sure on the warpath, how he's scattering around that the sheriff ain't doing anything to capture the desperate killer and jail breaker, and that for the safety of the public he will do his duty and sooner or later bring the criminal to justice himself.

"It ain't so long till election, and such talk spreading around some of the narrow-brains of the country is sure to hurt the sheriff's good reputation and cause him to lose many votes. Sammy reasons on that for a few days, figures out his own chances and then writes the constable to come and get him or send railroad fare and he'd come back himself. But the constable don't come thru with his bluff and don't send no railroad fare. Instead, a few days later two strange officers come to the outfit and arrest Sammy. All this is done without the sheriff knowing, because the constable is figuring some way of getting the whole credit for the arrest of the 'criminal.'

"Sammy gets a hint of that from the officers' talk and that makes him pretty peeved, so, when about twenty of the forty miles to town is covered and the officers are riding ahead a bit, he cuts the sowing at the one corner of the saddle skirt, and between the lining and the top leather is a little flat automatic which he's hid there long before and for just such emergency. With his emergency shooting iron pointing at the officers he tells 'em to stop, leave all their artillery on their horses and to get off of 'em. Then he tells 'em that from there on he's going on alone and that he'd be sure to report to the constable up north, and riding away with their two horses and artillery he says that they'll find 'em in town, at the livery stable.

"Sammy keeps to his promise, leaves the horses at the stable and then rides on. He rides on north for a

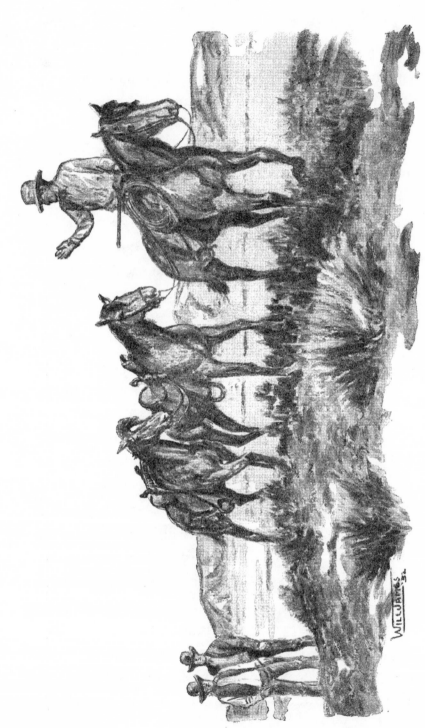

And riding away with their two horses and artillery he says that they'll find 'em in town.

hundred miles or so, leaving his horse rest only during the day, and finding a prospector's camp up high in the mountains he hides there for a week or so, till the rumors of his second escape dies down some. He rides another hundred miles on north and, coming to a little town along the railroad, he sells his horse and saddle and buys a ticket for the rest of the way north. He's anxious to have a few private words with the constable by then, and more than that.

"But his train ride ain't no more than half over when, as the train stops, he sees two men get on. They're the two officers he'd set afoot a while back and he knows daggone well they're still on his trail. So, when the train pulls out he steps off of it, hits for the outskirts of town and where he figures on locating a stable. He has no trouble doing that. Then he buys a half broke horse and a cheap saddle and hits out for the tall timber once more. But before leaving town he borrows some writing paper from the stable man, writes a letter and asks him to mail it for him. The letter is addressed to the constable.

"I don't remember exact what the letter says but I hears often afterwards that it's to the effect that Sammy is on the way, how he might arrive any day or maybe not for a month or so, but he would arrive sure enough, and arrive alone, and he would see that the constable is alone too before he shows himself.

"Sammy rides on north, hiding in the rough country by day and riding along valleys by night. He sends another letter on his way up, saying for the constable not to be lonesome, that he'll soon be there, and keeps on riding.

"The constable is getting sort of nervous by now. He don't know just when the little hook-nosed devil might pop up in front of him and he don't at all hanker to be alone when that time comes. A week goes by from the time he receives the first letter, then another week and another letter. A third letter comes and he notices by the postmarks on each that he's getting closer and closer. He's beginning to lose his appetite by then, he gets jumpy and his nerves are on hair trigger, like as if there's a ghost keeping step with him and waiting for a chance to choke the life out of him, and when one day he receives a fourth letter with the postmark of the town he's in and saying that Sammy had arrived and would see him sometime soon, that got to be too much for him. He don't only resign from office but he takes his belongings and family and quits the country.

"Sammy don't hear about that till some days later when he pays a visit to the sheriff, and the sheriff don't know what makes his 'trusted' constable resign and skip the country. But when the two get together and talk things over the whole thing is mighty plain, as to how come Sammy breaks jail and the constable quitting the flats so sudden. Both has to laugh over the whole thing, of course, and not only them but most everybody in the whole county and other counties around. The story spread like grass fire in a strong wind and the constable has to move a long ways to keep from feeling the heat.

"Sammy is 'jailed' again, the door is left unlocked and he eats at the Elite Chop House. When he gets a hearing he's cleared of the killing on grounds of self defense, and far as the jail breaking that's not brought up at all. The last time I sees him he's riding for the same outfit where he got in trouble with the cook."

The rider was quiet for a spell, and then he added on: "Every time I think of that little feller trying so hard to play square by them that was square with him, and then being aggravated by the devilment of others, I can see it was just pure luck or Providence that he didn't turn out to be just as bad as he's been good. He sure had the makings to be either."

CHAPTER SIX

THE KIDS DIDN'T WAKE UP for the antelope corralling and the rabbit egg gathering. They slept right on past three o'clock and it was four hours later before they blinked an eye. Uncle Frank and his riders was many miles away by then.

The bunk house stories came back to 'em as they got up, washed and went to breakfast and Martha was asked some questions about 'em while they et. She smiled at some of the stories that was repeated to her, but she agreed that the one about Sammy could easy be true for she knowed of stranger things happening on the range, even amongst her own kin.

Breakfast over with they ambled down to the corrals. Uncle Bill was nowhere in sight, but some horses was and they went to looking 'em over and trying to recognize the ones they'd rode the day before. They both was doing a little arguing as to which ones it was, and they'd finally come to agree on two of the horses when Uncle Bill's "good morning" was heard, and then they learned that neither of their horses was in the corral.

"I figured on giving you a change of horses for to day," he says. Then he asks, "And why am I doing that . . . ?"

*Trying to recognize the ones
they'd rode the day before.*

They both thought hard for a spell. Kip spoke first.
"I know. It's because you said that the more we change
to different horses the quicker we'll learn how to ride."

"Correct. And now I expect you two'll want to go
riding, or are you stiff and sore from yesterday's ride?"

One look at 'em was plenty of answer to that. The
old cowboy grinned, went to get his rope, while the kids
get their bridles, and soon had two horses caught for
'em.

"You're going to start learning how to saddle your
own horse to day," he says, "because a cowboy sure don't
have nobody do that for him."

Taking holt of his horse's reins he started on with
the teaching. "Now you watch me and I'll coach you

along some more later. First," he says, "remember to always hang on to your bridle reins when you saddle up, no matter how gentle your horse is or how well he stands, because you might not always be riding that kind and even a gentle horse might leave you afoot if you're saddling outside a corral. Another good habit to get into is to keep by his shoulder, for, if it's a mean horse, he might reach up with a hind foot and kick you. Of course with gentle horses like I caught you there's no such danger, but it's a mighty good idea to do as I'm telling you with any kind of a horse.

"Holding your reins with your left hand you reach for your saddle blanket with your right and when it's halfway up to his back you can give your reins a little slack and use both hands so it'll spread smooth. You want to make sure there's no dirt or twigs or wrinkles in the blanket because that'll cause a sore, and you also want to make sure that it reaches from the top of the withers to the hip bones, hanging even on both sides, and that the blanket is big enough so none of the saddle skirting will touch the horse's hide and rub the hair off.

"That done, you get your saddle by sticking the fingers of your right hand in the hole of the fork, lift it up that way, and giving the reins enough slack so you won't jerk your horse as you raise the saddle on his back. You also use your left hand to swing the cinches and stirrup over first, and holding your saddle up a bit so it won't shove the blanket off you bring it over his back and so it'll

WILLJAMES '32

Use your left hand to swing the cinches and stirrups over first.

come down straight. The front of the fork should come to about center of the withers."

After fitting the saddle so it set well he went on to show 'em how to cinch it up. He told 'em to be careful there's no twist in cinches or latigoes nor no saddle strings up in 'em, and that all should lay smooth and flat against the horse's hide. He drawed up the cinches (they was the buckle cinch and no complicated knot had to be tied in the latigo), and he explained how the front cinch should be the tightest, but not too tight, just so the saddle feels solid enough and so it'll stay put. The back cinch shouldn't be tight and about the only use there is to it is to keep the saddle from tipping up when roping.

Uncle Bill saddled and unsaddled his horse a couple of times, just to teach the kids how it was done and then they went to their own saddles and horses to try and do the same. But they got pretty well mixed up from the start. They held their reins too tight or too loose. Their lighter saddles was still too heavy for 'em and the horses was too high and every time they'd get a saddle up they'd push the blanket off the horse's back.

The old cowboy had to laugh as he coached 'em along, and they laughed right with him. The fun kept up with the teaching for a good half hour, and finally, with Uncle Bill's help, the saddles was put on right and cinched to stay.

"Of course the horses are a little big for you kids," he says, as the first saddling lesson was over, "and the saddles are a little heavy, too, but you'll get to learn how to saddle up your horses plenty good before summer is over. All that takes is a lot of practice.

"Now let's see if you two still remember what I learned you in how to get on your horses. I'm not going to say any more than I have to and only when you make mistakes, but I'll be watching you. So, go to it now, but take your time so you won't get all mixed up."

They took their time, and they got mixed up some. Uncle Bill hardly said a word. He just watched 'em and gave 'em a chance to figure things out by their own selves, and when either Kip or Scootie got on their horses and didn't do it right he'd tell 'em to get off and do it over again. Sometimes he'd have to tell 'em what it was they didn't do right, but not before he was sure they'd forgot, and after making 'em get on and off their horses about half a dozen times each he figured it enough for them.

He took the lead out of the corral, and he was pleased to notice that the kids well remembered how to start their horses and hold the reins. They also remembered when to pull or give slack while at different gaits and how to neckrein for turns.

"If you kids keep on as good as you're starting," says Uncle Bill, after watching 'em for a spell, "I'll be able to trust you to ride out by yourselves in a month or so . . . and you'll learn to sit in your saddles quicker and better if you quit hanging on the saddle horn, you've got it about choked blue now."

The kids laughed. "I thought that's what it was for," says Kip, "just a handle to hang on with."

It was Uncle Bill's turn to laugh. "Well," he says, "you're a little bit right at that, and some beginners or riders that ain't very good do grab a hold of it to keep from getting bucked off. But it ain't there for that purpose, the main use for it is to tie your rope onto when you're roping an animal, or any other work where the rope is used. It's also used to help get on a horse with, for hanging things on that's needed or picked up along the trail. The saddle horn has many uses and is very necessary in the cowboy's work, but never as a handle by any good rider, not if he can help it."

"Did you ever grab the horn to keep from getting bucked off, Uncle Bill?" Scootie asks.

"Yes, when I was a kid, and my dad sure used to rap my hand with his quirt too every time he caught me doing it."

The main use for it is to tie your rope onto when you're roping an animal.

"I guess he was the one who taught you how to ride, wasn't he?"

"Well, yes. He often used to take me up on his horse with him before I was big enough to walk, and we'd take long rides that way. I guess that started me to riding natural and without me realizing it, besides I was around horses and riders all the time, and when my dad handed me a horse for my own use he just handed him to me and told me to get in the middle of him and get to riding. I guess I was about four years old at the time."

As he talked, Uncle Bill noticed that both kids had let go of their holt on the saddle horn. "Let's trot our horses a bit now and see if you can do that without grabbing the horn again. You'll ride better if you do."

They done as they was told, and they was wondering at first if they would stay on their horses. They bounced up and down and everywhere and it was mighty hard for 'em to keep from grabbing the horn that was in front of 'em and so handy. They had to touch it a few times when they bounced too high, but as the pace was kept up they gradually settled to it some and finally they begin to believe that they really could ride better and easier when not hanging on.

But they grabbed for the horn again when the trotting pace changed to a lope. That change was a little bit too much for 'em, and they had to ride quite a ways at that gait before they felt confident enough to let go of their holt.

The gait was slowed down as the three got in rougher country, sometimes to a walk or "dog trot" (slow trot) and talking begin to take the lead again.

"Well, I'm going to start you kids to punching cows today," says Uncle Bill. "That's about the best way for you to learn how to ride good."

The kids looked at him, both wondering what he meant, and then Scootie asks:

"Punching cows? . . . But where's the sticks to punch them with, and what do we want to punch them for?"

The old cowboy grinned at Scootie and then says: "I guess I'll have to explain things a bit. . . . When we say punching cows we mean all the works that goes on with handling cattle, like rounding 'em up, branding, herding, trail driving and all that's done with the raising, caring and shipping of 'em. It takes in all the work a cowboy or cowpuncher does. The word cowpuncher was first fastened onto fellers who worked in the stock yards when the first shipments of wild cattle was made from Texas. That was about the time when your granddad was born. Them stock yard fellers used sticks and punched the cattle thru the loading chutes into the cars, and there's where the name cowpuncher first come in. They was called cowpunchers. Some of the young fellers went to riding on the range afterwards and the name stuck to 'em and sort of spread thru the cow country.

"The name 'cowboy' came before cowpuncher did and was first fastened onto kids who used to watch over little bunches of gentle cattle so they wouldn't stray away and mix in with the wild cattle that the Texas prairies was full of. That was before range cattle was worth anything. The range cattle then was the longhorn kind and wild as deer, and when there come a time that their hides was worth something they was hunted and shot just like deer. Then when a railroad was built towards the West a ways is when the wild cattle got to be worth some money, not only for the hides but for the meat too. The little cowboys who'd been riding barefooted and herding their dad's gentle cattle had now growed up, and the name 'cowboy' stuck on 'em as they went to gathering, trailing and shipping big herds of the wild cattle.

"That was the start of the first American cowboy."

Uncle Bill had been squinting away off in the distance as he spoke, and now he raised a hand towards where he'd been squinting. "I see a bunch of cattle out there," he says, sort of half to himself, "and I think it's the bunch I been missing lately."

The kids could see bunches of cattle everywhere but where he was pointing, and Kip told him so. "I can't see any cattle there," he says.

The old cowboy rode close to him and the horses was stopped, then he pointed again towards where his range trained eyes spotted the cattle. "Sight along my finger," he says, "and you'll see some cattle out there."

Kip sighted for a spell and said he did see something. Then Scootie sighted and finally located the objects too. "But," she says, "how do you know those specks are cattle? They might be horses."

"You can tell by the way they graze and move. Cattle graze further apart than horses and they move slower while grazing. Then cattle make a sort of square speck and highest at the rump, while horses make more of a round speck and are highest at the front."

That was easy enough to understand, but them specks away out there was still just specks to the kids, with no shape and no bigger than a pin head. Their eyes, as good or maybe better than Uncle Bill's, wasn't used to locating live objects on the range and the old cowboy, after his many years at hunting stock, could spot cattle or horses at one glance that they would never see even if they looked for them.

"But," says Kip, after the horses was started on again, "if those specks out there are cattle what makes you think they're the ones you've been missing? There's lots more cattle over there and the bunch you've missed might be amongst them."

"That's true enough, Son, but I'm pretty sure that that bunch is either stray cattle from some other range or the bunch I been looking for which strayed away and came back. I can see they ain't been here long."

That was sure a puzzle to the kids. How could he tell at that distance what kind of cattle they was, and Scootie had to ask him.

"Well, if they'd been here long they wouldn't be feeding where they are. The grass is just rank there and besides they're further away from water than cattle usually go. . . . Let's ride a little faster and get a close look at 'em."

In their excitement to get the closer look and see if Uncle Bill had guessed right the kids had forgot to grab the horn as they started their horses into a fast trot. The old cowboy had watched 'em and grinned to himself. He noticed too that they didn't bounce so much in their saddles either and that for the little riding experience they had they were sure getting into it fast.

Their eyes was straight ahead and on the specks that kept a getting bigger. After a while they could see for themselves that them specks was sure enough cattle, and being so anxious to see if Uncle Bill was right in his guessing about the cattle being the missing ones they sort of forgot about watching their riding. They just rode, and a heap better than when they did watch.

"Yep, that's the bunch I been missing," says Uncle Bill as they got to within half a mile of the cattle.

"How can you tell from here?" asks Kip.

"I recognize a 'marker' in the bunch."

"What's a marker?"

"A marker is an animal that's sort of odd in color or spots and which a rider remembers after seeing once. I remember seeing this marker before I missed the bunch and he was with it. That's how I know it's the same bunch."

And it was. They rode on closer, and as Uncle Bill looked the cattle over he acted sort of surprised. So did the kids when he spoke.

"By Japers," he says, "they been away over to Stink-ing Springs, and that's more than fifty miles from here. . . . Somebody's been trying to get away with 'em sure."

"How do you know they've been there," asks Scootie, "and what makes you think somebody's been trying to get away with them?"

"Look at the black dried mud sticking to their hocks. Stinking Springs is the only place that I know of where there is such dirt and I know this range for a hundred miles any direction from here. Far as me knowing that these cattle was drove away by somebody, that's easy enough to figure out, because this valley here is about as good a part of the range as there is and Stinking Springs is about the worst. No cattle would go there of their own accord, and I know that your Uncle Frank has no reason to drive any cattle that way, it's off his range. That's how I'm sure somebody's been trying to steal this bunch."

"But what do you think made 'em let go of the cattle?" Scootie asks, after a while. "Do you think it was because they felt sorry?"

The old cowboy grinned. "Yes, Scootie, I think they bumped up against some riders that *made* 'em feel sorry, alright."

"What kind of riders?"

"Oh, any riders from neighboring outfits that would recognize the cattle, or stock detectives that's always on the lookout for rustlers, or maybe the sheriff and a posse was watching. Anyway, we'll get news about this sooner or later."

The three rode a little ways from the grazing cattle, then Uncle Bill got off his horse, squatted to the ground and watched them for a spell. The kids done the same, and the talk went on.

"Gee," says Kip, "I'd like to see some of these rustlers and gunmen that I've read about in books and seen in the movies."

"I would, too," says Scootie, "but I think I'd be afraid because they steal girls and carry them away in the hills on their horses. Then they shoot so many people, and are always so mean to poor old widow ladies who are trying so hard to save their ranches—I'd rather see the heroes, they're so good and clean looking, and honest, and they can shoot so well."

Uncle Bill was grinning. "I don't think I ever seen one of them hero fellers," he says. "I know some mighty good men, as good as ever was born, and come as near to being heroes as anybody could, but they look just like anybody else. Their whiskers grow too, their shirts get dirty and their boots ain't always shined up. I even heard some of 'em swear, seen 'em drink hard likker and get wild, cheat their friends at horse trading and card playing. . . . Yep, the best of men have their faults and the worst of 'em have their good points. They wouldn't be human if they didn't. Of course, as we all know, there's some men a heap better than others and come mighty near being the heroes that you read about or see in the movies.

"I've knowed a few of such a kind, men that had the nerve of a wolverine and could fight their weight in wildcats, honest as they make 'em, and some of 'em good looking too," he grinned at Scootie, "but here's the queer part of it when such men are gun fighters. They might be fighting for law and peace and riding the country of bad characters, but after they kill off a few of them bad hombres they get sort of hankering to kill more. They get to the point where they sometimes shoot when they don't have to, and kill men that ain't so bad.

"I remember reading something one time where a feller said, 'If you live by a sword you'll die by a sword,' or such like. I think that's pretty true and goes for guns too. For most gun fighters I knowed, no matter how well they could fight or whether they was for or against the law, went up in smoke by guns, some of 'em before they got well started and the most of 'em before their whiskers showed any gray."

"Gee, I'd like to see one of those gun fighters before he's dead," says Kip.

"They're scarce," says Uncle Bill, laughing, "but you've already seen a couple of 'em right there at the ranch that had plenty of gun fights."

Kip and Scootie looked at one another, all excited and surprised. Scootie was the first one to speak.

"But," she says, "I didn't see any of the cowboys carry a gun, only Uncle Frank."

"Yes, and in the few fights your uncle had he always took his gun off. He can shoot fast and well but he's not a gun fighter, and the reason he packs one is in case he runs acrost somebody trying to get away with some of his stock, or to take a shot at a wolf, put some suffering critter out of its misery and such like."

"But why don't the two cowboys you say are gun fighters carry their guns with 'em?"

"Well, they're sort of over their recklessness and they had sense enough to quit in time, and, like all cowboys, they still have their guns but they leave 'em alongside of their war-bags pretty well instead of their hips. The same as the cowboy who told the story about little Sammy Doyle at the bunk house last night. Nobody knows it but me, but you're both going to know it now, too, and we're going to keep that to ourselves. That cowboy *is* Sammy Doyle, and in the telling of his story he just changed it and the description of himself a little so he wouldn't be giving himself away. He's packing another name now so he won't be looked at as a gun fighter and he's leaving his gun to home so he won't be one."

"And about your rustlers, Scootie," he says, looking at the girl, "I never as yet seen a one that you would need to be afraid of. They'd most likely be more afraid of you than you would be of them, because ladies is not at all in their line and they'd think no more of

91

harming or stealing one than they would the star that guides 'em at night.

"There's a cowboy riding for your uncle now that was quite a 'long rope artist' at one time, and . . ."

"What's a long rope artist?" asks Kip.

"That's what we call rustlers once in a while, and by 'long rope' we mean that they're covering a heap of territory and taking long chances to get the stock they're after. Well, this cowboy I started telling you about was brought to trial for cattle-rustling a couple of times and he was lucky enough to get free both times. There's no doubt but what he was guilty, and guilty of other such doings that never was found out, but there never was enough evidence to convict him.

"You wouldn't believe me if I was to tell you which rider it is, Scootie, and you didn't seem to be a bit scared of him last night."

"My goodness," Scootie says, "I didn't know that Uncle Frank had such bad men riding for him."

"I wouldn't call them bad men, Scootie. They're a heap better than reckless fellers who never as yet done any harm and learned the lesson that it don't pay to be wild. They got over their foolishness and they're wiser and more dependable than the man who's never been a little bad, on account that they've already sowed their wild oats, reaped 'em and found out a plenty that there was nothing in the harvest but chaff and thorns. . . . They'll never hanker to do any more sowing of wild oats."

The old cowboy stood up. "Well," he says, "we done more talking than cowpunching, but there's plenty other times for that and now we better be hitting the breeze back for the ranch."

But there was one more question, and Scootie had to ask. "Did you ever steal any cattle, Uncle Bill, and were you ever a gun fighter?"

He grinned and shook his head. "That's not a question for little girls like you to ask," he said, "and not a question for an old man like me to answer."

W.J.

CHAPTER SEVEN

THERE WAS SOME HAPPY DAYS when the kids took on all they could of what the Five-Barb ranch and range could offer, and a whole lot like a cool mountain stream is to a thirsty rider. They rode here and there and most everywhere, and Uncle Bill would sometimes take some chuck along so they wouldn't have to ride back for the noon meal. The lunch wasn't made up of sandwiches nor any kind of fancy didos,—just flour and coffee each in a little sack, baking powder, salt and a hunk of bacon. All was stuck in an empty lard bucket. A tin plate and three tin cups was added and the whole thing was easy wrapped up in two slickers and tied behind two of the saddles, only a couple of extra pounds to each.

When the sun shot straight down, Uncle Bill would most always have a place located by some clear stream or spring and where there was plenty of shade and grass, sometimes by trout streams where the kids would fish for a few trout to go along with the bacon. Being they had no perticular place to go and was free to be where they wished, they had their pick of the best camping places. At such places is where they learned how the cowboy takes care of his horse while stopping that way, where and how he starts his fire and how he cooks his meal. They didn't get to experience how the cowboy makes out when he has to camp on the desert, without water, only rank salt grass for his horse, stunted sage to make a fire and cook a dry meal with and then going to sleep wondering if he'd find water on the next day. Nor did they get to experience how to make camp as the cowboy does while drifting thru snowbound country, half froze and grass all covered up, but while making camp at the different pretty places Uncle Bill located for 'em, he told 'em of them places where it wasn't so nice. He told 'em of some of his experiences that way. The kids would listen mighty close, and Kip acted like he wouldn't mind taking on some such experience. As for Scootie, she was more inclined to want water when she was thirsty and a big fire when she was cold, and, of course, plenty of good grass for her horse all the time.

"I stopped by a big dry wash one time," says Uncle Bill, telling of an experience of his one day noon, "that was in the big desert a long ways south of here. I'd been following that wash thinking I'd find some little pool of water in some of the hollowed rocks that was in the bottom of it. I was so dry that I'd chewed mud if I'd found some. My horse was ganted up and just as dry as I was and he wouldn't even put his head down to look for grass. He wasn't hungry, and it was just as well he wasn't because there was nothing for him to eat anyhow, nothing but little black twisted-up sage.

"In the back of my saddle I had some 'jerky' (dried beef or venison) and soda crackers, the best things to take when a man is traveling acrost country without a pack horse. It's light, and four or five pounds of that together will keep a cowboy in good shape for a week or more. But I didn't touch any of the jerky or crackers, because I wasn't hungry either.

"The more thirsty you are the less appetite you have, and even tho we'd been drifting steady, me and my horse was to the stage where we didn't have no appetite at all, for neither of us had touched moisture for about two days. I'd kept wallering a little pebble in my mouth to sort of keep what saliva I had left in me circulating and I didn't take the bridle off my horse on account that the bit in his mouth helped him the same way as the pebble did me."

He'd picked up one of the bridle bits that was near and showed the kids what good use a well-made bit was. "You see that little barrel-shaped wheel in the center of the mouth-piece? That's what we call a 'crickel' and it's there for a horse to waller over his tongue when he wants to. Them crickels are mighty fine for a horse that's ner-vous and figity, too. He'll roll it with his tongue and the sound it makes will help quiet him.

"The old U. S. Army bits had the best mouthpiece I ever seen. They was made something like this." He drawed the shape of 'em

The old U. S. Army bit mouth-piece.

in the dirt with a twig. "But I didn't like the side bars on them bits, they was too long and made the bit too severe.

"Well, to go on with the story, I didn't stop by the dry wash to eat, it was to rest while the heat was at its worst and save what strength me and my horse had for when it got cooler. There's one thing about the old desert. It might sizzle you during the day but it usually makes you wear a coat or reach for a blanket during the night.

"My horse went to sleep a-standing and I sort of dozed in the shade of him, but I didn't dare doze hard nor take on too much of the shade he made, because he was weaving like a willow to a breeze, and I was leary he might fall on me. I'd come out of my dozes sudden every once in a while and blink at the long distances of flat white and sizzling landscape all around me. Outside of far away low and dry hills that seemed hanging on air on account of the mirage that was between them and me, there wasn't a break in the whole land but the dry wash I was alongside of. I figured on hitting for the dry hills soon as it begin to get cooler, and I was hoping mighty strong that I would run acrost some trail on the way, some trail made by hoofs of antelope or wild horses, because then I'd know there'd be water in them hills and all I'd have to do is follow the trail to wherever it was."

Here Scootie interrupted with a question. "Didn't you have a canteen of water along with you?" she asked.

"No. I never seen a cowboy pack a canteen on his saddle. It flops too much and he figures it an awkward and unnecessary weight. He'll laugh at anybody who packs one and class him as a tenderfoot. Another thing is the sentiments every good cowboy has for his horse, and being he can't take enough along for him, he'll go without it too, and save him that extra weight. It's only when he has a pack horse along that he might add on a canteen if the pack is light, but seldom even then.

My horse went to sleep standing and I sort of dozed in the shade of him.

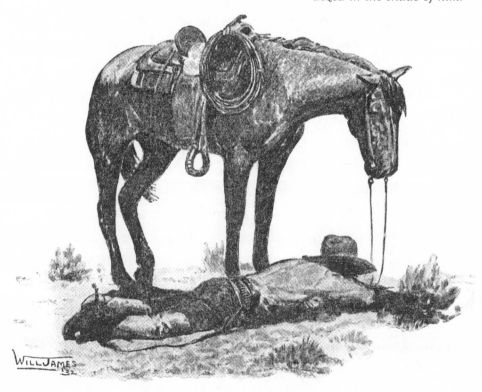

"The desert rider is used to going a long time without water, or without anything to eat, and if he's pretty sure of striking a camp where he'll get grub within twenty-four hours, he won't take even a bite along. It's only when going on a many days' ride and don't figure on stopping at any camp, or ranch, that he'll take anything to eat, and then he'll most likely have a pack horse and take his bedding along too. I've read and heard tell of cowboys sleeping in their saddle blankets, that's true enough and most every cowboy has had to often enough, but that goes better in a story than it does in life. If he can, the cowboy will have his tarpaulin covered bedding to crawl into when comes his chance to rest.

"It's only when he's in a heap of a hurry that he'll leave his pack horse behind, and then, if he's going on a long trip, he'll just roll up a half dozen pounds of jerky and biscuits or bannock mixed and tie it on his saddle. He won't take no flopping canteen, not even tho he knows he might sometime wish that he had.

"I was mighty thirsty that day when I stopped along that dry wash, but I never thought of a canteen because I'd never packed one. Finding a hoof mark is all that was in my mind, that would be a sign there was water somewhere and maybe not too far away. It seemed a mighty long time since I'd seen a hoof mark of any kind, only when I'd doze a bit during the heat of the day, then I'd see 'em in my dream.

"The sun was hitting for the west and beginning to lose some of its heat when I stood up and blinked at the ocean of land around me. I stirred my tired and thirsty horse, and we both started slowly to putting one foot ahead of the other, me leading him. We must of gone about a mile, still following the wash, when I stopped short, thinking sure I was out of my head, for right by my boot toe was what looked like the print of an antelope's hoof in the hardpan dirt. And it was, but I had to feel of it with my fingers to make sure.

"Of course I knowed that antelope often go a long ways from water, and this hoof print I seen might of been twenty miles from any, but it was sure encouraging to see that something alive had been where I was and had kept on going with its carcass, even if it was a speedy antelope. I talked to my horse about it, tried to make him look at the dim hoof print, and wished he'd understand what the sight of it meant.

"The sight of that hoof print sure brought new life to me, and I went as crazy to looking for more as a prospector goes crazy when he finds his first flake of gold. I found more hoof prints, zigzagging all directions, which showed that the antelope had just been roaming around and headed for no perticular place. But I knowed that them tracks would sooner or later get in with some others and finally lead me to water if I followed 'em. I sure followed 'em, and my nose near touched the ground as I did because I feared of losing sight of 'em. The tracks got more plentiful as I went and that was sure encouraging, but as I'd straighten up and look around once in a while it sure looked hopeless of there being any water closer than where the low hills was, and I knowed that the hills was at least thirty miles away.

"Then, as I followed the antelope tracks, I got another surprise that made me rub my eyes and look a few times. It was the hoof print of a horse, and further on was more of 'em. Now I knowed that horses seldom go over ten or fifteen miles from water. I seen more horse tracks. I picked up speed and after a while I come to a plain trail where there was lots of horse and antelope tracks.

"The trail was easy to follow now and I didn't have to keep my nose to the ground any more, but as I looked over the country ahead, I couldn't see any sign of where there could be water to within any ten or fifteen miles, even if there was plenty of horse tracks on the trail. I got on my horse to get a little higher view, rode along for a few miles, and then I got the sudden sight of what looked like a bunch of overgrown antelope. They was antelope sure enough. I could see their white rumps shining to the sun, and the mirage, acting like a magnifying glass, is what made 'em look so big, about the size of a horse. Further on beyond 'em was some horses and they looked about the size of elephants.

"At the sight of the antelope and the way they was bunched, I made my weaving horse walk a little faster, for it looked to me like them antelope was drinking.

"It seemed to take a mighty long time to cover the distance to where the antelope was, and to help my horse I got off of him and walked some more. I was even pulling him, and the poor devil was so all in that he didn't see the antelope that only walked away when I got to within a few hundred yards of 'em.

"I can't begin to describe to you kids how I felt when as I looked at the closest of the antelope I seen drops

At the sight of the antelope and the way they was bunched, I made my weaving horse walk a little faster.

of water dripping from their chins. In the sun them drops looked like diamonds and to me they looked a heap more precious than any diamond. But where was the water hole? . . . the land was flat, not a hollow nowhere. My heart sort of went up my throat some as I kept on walking and looking, thinking that maybe I was sure out of my head this time. Then as I made another step I come near walking over it, the water hole.

"It was a sure enough water hole, and I could never find out or guess how deep it was, but the top of the hole was only about the size of a horse's hoof print. Clear water was bubbling up in it in a way that reminded me of drinking fountains I've seen in towns. None of the water flowed out of the hole, just bubbled like coming up for air and churned back underground. By that and the depth of the hole I figured that water to be from a big underground river, maybe a mile below.

"You can bet your boots that I didn't stop to do any figuring as to where that water came from when I first spotted it. I didn't even stop to think that it might be poisonous. If I had, the antelope was enough proof that it wasn't. There was signs that they'd been watering there regular and I couldn't see no bleached bones nowheres around. Anyhow, I scooped up a handful of that water and splashed it on my horse's nostrils, and if I ever seen a horse come out of it sudden it was him. I splashed some more over his eyes and head and then, leaving the bit in his mouth so I could hold him and so he wouldn't gulp so fast, I let him have a few sips. I had to be mighty careful not to let him have too much at once or it might of killed him.

"After I let him have his first few sips I held him back with one hand while I used the other to splash water over my own head and face. I spit out my pebble and wallered water now instead of it. Then I gargled some, and finally I swallowed a couple of sips myself. My tongue wasn't swelled much, but I went easy on that water just the same at first.

"The thirst being sort of checked up some, I led my horse away from the water so the sight of it wouldn't be too much of a temptation. I sure wasn't going to go very far, not for quite a spell. But I didn't get much further than a hundred yards away from the water hole when I found another of the exact same kind and size. Then I looked towards the horses that was a couple of miles away and they acted like they was drinking out of another of the natural fountains. I scooped a couple of swallows out of the second hole, let my horse have a few more sips, and then went on to where the bunch of horses was. Another water hole was there sure enough, and I thought I must of been following in line with the underground river.

"But now it looked like this hole was the last one where the underground river came to the top and I didn't get very far away from it. If there'd been any grass around for my horse, I'd stayed there all night, but there's never no feed of any kind close to water in the desert because the stock always graze that off first, as they leave the water.

"The sun went down, the air got nice and cool and then, after taking on some more water, I begin to feel normal again and my appetite soon came back. I chewed on some jerky and crackers while wishing there was something for my horse to eat, for he was fast beginning to feel normal too, and hungry enough so he nibbled at the dry sage.

"I guess it was along about midnight when I let my horse have all the water he wanted. He was hungry but he was pretty strong again. He had a good rest and lost his weaving walk. I took on all I could hold of water, got on my horse, and for the first time in my life I wished I had a canteen to take some along.

"But I wouldn't of had much need for a canteen from then on because as early morning come, after I'd crossed the low hills, I seen the dim outline of mountains against the sky, and when the sun came up to shine on 'em they looked awful good, for I seen they was covered with timber. There was quaker in the canyons and that meant water there and bunch grass on the hillsides. It was just getting good and hot again when my horse splashed ankle deep in a cool little stream which we both took a drink out of and then we went on up it into the cool shade of the quakers where I unsaddled and *sure made camp.*

"I left my horse loose up on the side of the hill and where he could bury his head up to his eyes in bunch grass. He wouldn't leave because he was sure ready to make camp too."

The old cowboy had come to the end of his story and everything was quiet for a spell. Kip stared away off in the distance and then he finally said, "Gee, Uncle Bill, I wish I'd been with you."

CHAPTER EIGHT

THERE WAS SELDOM a noon hour stop made
when the old cowboy didn't tell of some of his
experiences while camping in different parts of the range
country. He'd seen many parts of it before he settled
down to riding for the Five-Barb, parts where it got to
sixty below zero in winters, and other parts to the south
where it was sixty above zero at that same time of the
year. His rambling trail had covered thousands of miles
of range land. He'd camped alongside of snowdrifts,
other times where canyons was like red hot furnaces,
and as he went to telling of his experiences, it was in
a way that'd be a sort of teaching to the kids so that
no matter where they camped they'd get an idea of what
to do, how and when to travel, how to go by signs on
land and sky, and how to take care of themselves and
their horses.

"There's one thing you got to remember all the time,"
he kept a-repeating to 'em, "and that's to take good care
of your horse. I seen fellers ride a horse as tho he was
a machine, but them fellers has never been anywhere
nor ever learned what a horse is. They never stop to
think that a horse has feelings, that he might be sore-

His rambling trail had covered thousands of miles of range land.

footed or tired. They'd learn them things plenty quick if they was set afoot a few times and have to pack their belongings and themselves for any long distance. Men have gone a long ways afoot and packed heavy loads, like the prospector and trapper for instance, but they learn to take care of themselves mighty well. They won't run up a hill when they're tired, if a shoe hurts 'em they'll stop and fix it, and if the pack don't set right they'll fix that too. And so, if you're traveling a-horse-back you ought to take care of your horse as much as you do of yourself, and more, because he's the one that's packing you and he's got as much feelings as you have, even tho he don't cry about it like us humans do. He'll suffer along, do his best, and even die for some daggone fool and ignorant humans he's packing or carting around.

"If you're riding along, just for the fun of it, and your horse is in good shape I wouldn't lope or run him over a mile at a time, nor trot him over a couple of miles. I'd break his gait pretty often and according to the roughness of the country, and I'd let him walk most of the time in any country.

"When a cowboy hits out for a two or three hundred mile ride on a fat horse that's not hardened in, he'll start him out pretty easy on the first day, specially if it's hot, and he won't go over thirty miles if he can help it. He might go a little further the next day, and if he's hitting out on a thousand mile trip and wants to save his horse he'll never go over forty miles a day. The cowboy's pet gait for a long trip is the 'running walk.' That's between a fast walk and a slow trot. A heap of distance can be covered in a day at that gait."

As usual, the kids had many questions to ask as the old cowboy talked and told 'em different stories and things, and being most always somewhere in the hills with 'em when such talks went on, he had a good chance to show and explain what he meant.

Like, for instance, "When you stop for noon, to rest your horse or to camp for the night," he'd said once, "you always want to see to your horse first because it takes him longer to eat than it does you. If you're stopping for any length of time take the saddle off, or at least loosen the cinch and raise the saddle a few times to air his back. If you have a pack horse along you want to do the same for him. A pack will gall a horse quicker than a saddle and a hundred pounds of the dead weight is as hard on him as a two-hundred-pound rider is to a saddle horse. The dead weight don't give, it shifts and bounces, and when stopping for any length of time or to make camp the pack horse should be relieved of his load first, before the saddle horse is unsaddled."

Then he'd went on to show the kids how to let their horses graze without running chances of having them get away.

"There's some horses you can trust to let graze by just dropping the bridle reins or lead rope, some that you can take the bit out of their mouths, leaving the bridle around their necks and letting the reins drag. That's only for short stops, and you've got to know something about horses, specially about the one you're riding, before dropping the reins, or he might leave you. A horse is more apt to leave you if he's not very hungry or tired, or if the grass is scarce and he's not very far away from home. If your horse is fresh and you're not going far nor stopping long, it's best to tie him up and not let him graze. When you tie him up you should use the lead rope of your hackamore, or if you haven't got a hackamore, tie a rope around his neck. Be sure the knot won't slip, then run one end of the rope thru the curb strap of the bit and tie him to something solid, not to a post or a wire fence if you can help it, for he might paw over the wire and cut himself. And don't tie him too long or too short, just long enough so if he puts his head down he won't get a foot over the rope.

"Most of our horses will stand or graze when the reins or lead rope is dropped to the ground, but all of 'em get wise to the dragging of 'em in time, and if they're in mind to, or something scares 'em, they can make a get away without hardly stepping on 'em. Some will get away quicker than others, and some won't try, but it's always best to get to know your horse well before dropping the reins, unless you want to take the chance of being left afoot.

"Many cowboys carry hobbles on their saddles all the time. They're light and made of twisted rawhide or plain leather and if a horse is not to be trusted, the hobbles are fastened on his front feet, the same while saddling if he begins to act up too much. But horses get wise to hobbles, too, and some will travel many miles in one night if the feed is scarce, if they're thirsty or if they want to get back to wherever they left.

"Hobbles are used pretty well everywhere by the drifting cowboy of the range countries, but more so where the sagebrush is thick and where feed is scattering, like in parts of the southern states. And the cowboy is mighty perticular as to how he puts the hobbles on his horses when he stops to make camp for the night. He'll see that they're on to stay, and he'll also see that they won't make any sores. Sores can easy be made if the hobbles ain't put on right and if they're too tight. They'll make sores even then if they're left on too long, and sometimes cause a horse to limp pretty bad. So, a cowboy never hobbles a horse unless he just has to.

"In grass countries, like here for instance, and where there's not much brush only in the mountains, most horses are broke to the picket rope before they are to the saddle. The regular picket rope for unbroke horses is a heavy one-inch soft-twisted rope and about forty feet long. One end is fastened to the hackamore or halter, and the other to a log heavy enough to hold a horse and not too heavy so he can't drag it a little. A well broke picket horse will never tangle himself up in the rope and he can be picketed with any kind of a rope without burning himself.

"The picket rope is better than hobbles for a horse *if he's broke to it* and if there's plenty of grass. When you look for a picketing place for the night you want to make sure there's no snags that might catch the rope and hold the horse in one little spot all night and where he won't have a chance to graze. A horse should never be picketed where there's brush. That's why few horses are picket-broke in sage brush countries, and mostly hobbles are used.

The regular picket rope for unbroke horses is a heavy, one-inch, soft-twisted rope and about forty feet long.

"Now, if you camp to a place where there's no log handy to picket your horse to, the top branches of a willow will do near as well, if you tie the rope high enough so there'll be some give in case the horse jerks on the rope. But with a well broke and gentle picket horse you can picket him to anything solid if you want. A tree or a peg in the ground will do, only be sure he's well picket-broke before you do that or he might get tangled up and hurt himself. The safest way to find out is to ask whoever knows the horse, and if you ain't got the chance to do that, try him out with a long soft and thick rope and picket him to something he can drag but can't run away with. Don't never picket or tie a horse by the neck either, because if the knot is not tied right it might slip and he might choke himself. Always use a hackamore or a halter."

"What's a hackamore?" Kip asked one day, as him and Scootie was being coached to the ways of picketing a horse.

"A hackamore is a combination of braided rawhide, cotton rope and leather. There's a nose band of braided rawhide that's called 'Bosal,' which is held up in place by a light piece of leather over the head. Then a doubled cotton rope that ties around the neck and fastens to the bosal under

A hackamore is a combination of braided rawhide, cotton rope and leather.

114

the chin, that's called a 'Feador,' and in the making of it is two of the most complicated knots a man ever invented. A hackamore is twice as light and strong as a halter, less awkward and is used a lot in breaking horses."

Scootie was a whole lot interested in the goings on of hobbling, picketing and taking care of a horse while in the hills, but not as much as Kip, because maybe she never figured on drifting around by her lonesome as Kip might some day. But she beat Kip in watching Uncle Bill while camp was being set and things was started to cooking, and after her and Kip had been showed how to build a fire she'd fast learned how to make a hand of herself in helping with the meal.

She remarked one time that they ought to have another little bucket to cook things in, and some knives and forks and a frying pan.

"They'd be handy alright," Uncle Bill had said, "but they'd be more load for a horse to pack, and if you was to go a long long ways you'd soon be throwing all them extra things away so as to help him. I'm only showing you how we camp in the hills now, Scootie, and if a feller can't get along without a lot of things, he'd better take a pack horse or else stay home."

"And," she'd went on, "I don't like coffee without cream or sugar, either."

Uncle Bill laughed. "Well," he said, "there's water in the creek, and it's just as good if you don't like black coffee and the weather ain't too cold."

The setting of camp was pretty simple and after the old cowboy coached 'em a few times they learned that easy enough. After the horses was tended to, a spot to build a fire was picked out. It was a dangerous country to build a fire in, the grass was tall and the last year's growth was heavy. Trees was thick, fallen dry limbs was mixed in with the grass and underbrush, and all was just like ready for a little spark that would turn that grassy timbered mountain land into a black desert of coal and ashes.

The old cowboy done his best to explain the dangers of building a fire in such a country, and what a little spark might do if it got to the underbrush and pine needles. "You see all them fine big trees?" he said, pointing up the mountain. "They're sure pretty, ain't they? That stream is sure pretty, too, ain't it? And that tall grass in the valley below is mighty fine. Well, them fine big trees have a heap to do with all of that, and if one little spark got away, started a fire amongst 'em and turned 'em into black stumps, that pretty stream there would just about dry up, and the fine grass in the valley below would hardly come up.

"Why? Because they make a wind break and hold the snow. The wind can't blow it away once it lights, and it lays heavy amongst 'em. Them trees will hold the snows and store it during winters and protect it from the hot sun during summers. Protected that way it'll keep all summer in some places. The mountains are kept full of moisture by the slow melting snow, the streams and springs are kept a-running and spreading more moisture to the valley, and there's grass everywhere, fat cattle and horses and wild animals and birds.

"Burn them trees off and the snow sweeps on over the mountains, banks up only in the canyons and coulees and is not protected from the sun. It melts with the first warm days of spring, high water washes away the land, cuts it up, and the grass roots go on to the river and then the ocean. When summer comes and moisture is needed for the grass in the valleys, the mountain is as dry and bare as the valley is, cattle and horses drift away to other ranges and so does wild animals and birds. It's worse than a desert. It's dead land, black and with carcasses of burned animals scattered over it. It would take many years for it to come back to life.

"And just think," went on the old cowboy, as him and the kids looked at the big trees and grass covered ridges, "it only takes a little spark to do the transforming."

That went pretty deep into the kids' hearts and they was mighty careful to watch Uncle Bill as he picked out a place to build the fire. He warned 'em never to build it near a tree nor under any hanging limbs, specially of a pine tree, because the needles of any kind of pine are always full of pitch and it's as dangerous to have heat near 'em as if they was soaked with gasoline.

He picked out an open space, close to the creek, away from down timber and where the ground was free from dry timber rot so there'd be no danger of the fire tunnelling under and reaching thick brush without being seen. Then he gathered a couple of handfuls of dry pine needles and one armful of dry limbs which he put over the top of 'em. One little match to the pine needles started the fire. It was a pretty good size fire but it was in a safe place, and all that was done for the time being was to watch the grass that was burning around it and keep the grass fire from spreading by hitting the flames with a stick. When a fair size circle of grass was burned off, the camp fire was called safe enough so long as flying sparks or coals was watched.

The cowboy never builds a rock fireplace to cook on nor a frame of sticks to hang pots from while making camp (but the rock fireplace is the safest, specially when the camper is not experienced). He'll make a good size fire, watch it while it burns down to coals and does his cooking with his kettles flat on the hot coals, never on flames. That way he can cook close to his fire without getting smoked up or singed, and if the coals get cold he'll add on a few little dry twigs around the pot or under the pan to liven 'em up. Whenever anything is cooked and he wants to keep it hot, he smooths out a few coals on the side with a stick and leaves it on' em.

When the kids went on their first camp meal with Uncle Bill they wondered how he'd be able to cook much of anything with only a little bucket and a tin plate, and they watched him mighty close. While the fire was burning down to good coals he whittled out two sticks, one flat to mix a batter with, and the other pointed to use as a fork. He hunted up a flat rock, cleaned the top of it and set it near the fire to heat it a little and then he went to mix up a stiff batter in the little bucket, just flour, a little baking powder and a pinch of salt. He stirred that up good first, then added on a little water gradual and kept on a-stirring till he got the dough well mixed, about the same stiffness as bread dough and so it could be handled with the hands. That dough mixed, he rolled it in a big lump, took it out of the bucket and set it on the rock. Then the little bucket was washed out in the stream, filled about three-quarters full of water, set on the hot coals, and the coffee grounds emptied in while the water was still cold.

Then the tin plate was set on the coals, two slices of bacon put in it and while they melted into a little grease, a piece of dough was squeezed out of the main hunk on the rock and flattened in the tin plate with the back of the hand. The bacon was saved from too much cooking by setting it on top of the pan cake, or "bannack" as it's sometimes called. There's different ways of mixing and cooking bannacks.

Kip and Scootie liked the smell of the cooking mighty well, but after seeing how the pan bread had been mixed and cooked, even tho Uncle Bill had been mighty clean about it, they was a little dubious as to how it would taste. They'd never et such plain cooking and the variety of other things they'd been used to was sure lacking. But even tho the cooking was sure enough plain, the old cowboy sure knowed how to mix and cook it in a way that'd make highcrowned cooks quit. The grub wasn't so rich but there was a cleaner taste to it and a heap more fitting to the stomach, like mountain air sifting thru pines is to the lungs.

With his sharp stick, Uncle Bill turned the pancake over, and when it was done to a brown crisp he fished it out, broke it in two with his hands, remarking that hands was made before knives and forks, and handed the kids each a half with a piece of bacon stuck in the center. They was sort of careful in taking the first bite, but that was only for the first bite, and after that they'd fell victims to the plainest and tastingest grub they'd ever et.

Two more slices of bacon was put in the plate, another hunk of dough flattened out and cooking, and then the coffee came to a boil. It wasn't let boil long when it was drug off the fire a bit and then a little cold water, less than half a cupful, was sort of sprinkled on top to settle the coffee grounds to the bottom. Now the coffee was ready.

One bannack after another was divided around. Uncle Bill kept every second or third one for himself and et while he cooked, and when the last hunk of dough was

All three stretched out in the shade and eyes half closed watched their horses graze.

used and the last bannack disappeared, the kids had no thought for any other variety of grub or desert, and their tummies wouldn't of had room for any, not even their favorite.

There was lull in talk and action for a spell. All three stretched out in the shade, and eyes half closed, watched their horses graze. Kip and Scootie thought they never could eat bannack again for many days, but when the next day come, they was more than ready for their share again with the usual piece of bacon in the center.

Sometimes the old cowboy would add on a little variety in cooking the noon baits, like mixing a few raisins with the last round of bannacks to sort of take the place of desert, or he'd take along and cook a little rice too ("the horse-thief's special") and flavor it either with "sow belly" (salt pork) or raisins, then a few strings of jerky which was whittled off and et dry. Jerky can be cooked by just plain boiling, and adding on a little rice and bacon makes a pretty fair stew. But jerky takes a heap of boiling to get it tender and it's seldom cooked only when camp is made for the night and there's a lot of time to cook it in.

Them foods just mentioned are the cowboy's standby when he's traveling "light" (without pack horse) and going a long ways. He won't take the whole variety, just what's the lightest and he depends some on getting a shot at a cottontail rabbit, sage hen or grouse while on the trail to help keep up the grub supply.

The real-light traveling cowboy don't bother taking pot or pan. He mixes his bannack dough in a small sack, then dips it in water till he gets the right stiffness, and flattens it and cooks it on a rock that he's heated under a steady fire, just brushes the coals off the top and there's something like a hot stove. It'll keep the heat a long time with the coals around. Sometimes there's nothing but salt in them bannacks, no grease and no bacon, but as many a cowboy has proved they sure have a quality of keeping a rider in the saddle for a long ways.

It turned out to be Scootie's job to wash the little bucket and tin plate. That was done by the stream, in cold water, and sand was used for soap. All the black from the coals had to be sanded off after each meal so that everything else could be kept clean when tied to the saddle, and while she was busy at that, Kip and Uncle Bill was busy scraping the coals of the fire to a heap with sticks and pouring water on it. Then dirt was heaped on top to keep any coals or ashes from blowing away and coming back to life if a wind come up. Water was also poured on the dirt to make a heavy, smothering coating.

CHAPTER NINE

WITH THE MANY DAYS of riding and camping here and there, one time in the hills, another time in the valleys, by springs and creeks and rivers, and listening to the old cowboy's talk, Kip and Scootie got to the stage where nothing in the big range country was much of a surprise to 'em any more. Everything was just a pleasant something to learn, see and breathe in, and they had a nature trained teacher with 'em who sort of made the range land and all that lived in it like an open book. He'd point out many things they'd never got to see if they'd been by themselves and explained many other puzzling things they'd never understood.

They'd rode up on a little knoll one day and Uncle Bill's far-seeing eyes spotted a bunch of horses away off in the distance.

"There's some wild horses," he says, pointing.

"Wild horses?" says Kip, wondering, "I thought all the horses that are loose on the range were wild horses."

"Well," says Uncle Bill, "they're all sure enough wild, but there's two kinds, the range horse and the regular wild horse such as that bunch out there. The difference in 'em is size and breeding, and even tho the range horse is just as wild when corralled, and can fight and buck harder than the regular wild horse on account he's bigger and more hot-blooded, they're what we call 'herd-broke' which means that a cowboy can ride pretty close to a bunch while they're loose on the range. They might give the rider a good run, but they'll slow down in time and turn when he rides to one side or the other of the bunch. They might be hard to turn too, and hard to corral, once they're turned, but once the long fan-shaped wings on each side of the corral gate are reached, they can be run on in pretty well. The range horse is what we break and use for our work. It's seldom that we use what we call the wild horse. He might be a little easier to break, but as a rule he's too small and he's always got to be watched or he'll go back to the wild bunch.

"The regular wild horse, or mustang and cayuse, as some folks call 'em, are descendents of horses that some Spanish explorer brought from Spain a few hundred years ago. Some of 'em got away from the Spaniards and went wild and accumulated till come a time when wild horses was everywhere in the west. Them horses you see out there are of the same breed, only mixed in a little with some better horses that's brought in the west the last seventy years or so. But the mixing didn't seem to help 'em much. They're inbred and not many are what a cowboy would be proud of riding.

"So they're just let go. Some are trapped and caught and shipped to the East, and I guess that's how come

We leave the cayuses for the Indians.

WILL JAMES

that most Eastern folks think we ride cayuses out here. We leave the cayuses for the Indians.

"You can't corral a wild horse like you can a range horse. They'll run and keep on running the minute they see a rider, and a rider's got to be on a mighty fast horse to get near a bunch of 'em. When he does get near they won't turn, and if he crowds 'em they'll scatter past him like a bunch of quail and run to wherever they want to go.

"The only way to catch 'em is either to rope 'em or run 'em into a blind trap. A blind trap is a corral built in the timber or along rocky mountain rims, hid so that it'll look just like part of the country. It's also got to be where the horse will run natural because, as I said before, they only go where they want to. You couldn't get 'em into a corral that's in plain sight, not unless you roped every one and drug 'em in."

Uncle Bill was talking along when one of the wild horses spotted him and Kip and Scootie on the knoll. A wild horse can see a mighty long ways, and that one had no more than raised his head than the whole bunch did the same. Then they bunched up close, milled around a little, pretty soon a direction was decided on by a leader and the whole bunch lined out in a long lope, their long distance gait.

"You'd have a hard time catching up to 'em now," says Uncle Bill.

They'll scatter past him like a bunch of quail.

Kip and Scootie hardly took a breath as they watched the wild ones stir the dust acrost the valley in their smooth long lope. They looked mighty pretty and there was something about their wild action that gave 'em a strange feeling, like they was living at a time hundreds of years past.

They rode down off the little knoll, acrost a flat and then Uncle Bill headed for a tall mountain where he took the lead up a trail along a deep canyon. A clear little stream cut thru thick groves of quakers and made a thousand little falls over big boulders, making a noise so the sound of horse's hoofs on the trail could hardly be heard. The brush was thick on both sides of the trail and so was the timber along the rocky rims of the ridges.

They was riding along when Uncle Bill stopped his horse and made a motion with his hands for the kids to stop too and be quiet. Then he pointed down to the stream below and the kids got their first glimpse of deer outside of a zoo. They looked different in the open that way, and gave 'em a thrill they didn't get while looking at 'em behind bars. There was a buck, two does and a fawn, and when Uncle Bill rode on and showed himself the kids got to see the deer in action. They skipped and hopped over brush like they was on wings and hardly seemed to touch the ground. In a few seconds they was out of sight.

They seen a few more deer further up. Then high up along a rocky ledge the old cowboy pointed out a big horned mountain sheep. It was hard for the kids to locate the mountain sheep because it blended so well with the rocks, and when they finally did see it they more than wondered how Uncle Bill ever spotted it in the first place. They wondered too, as they rode along, why he didn't shoot at the deer or the mountain sheep. He was packing a rifle on his saddle that day.

Kip finally had to ask him. And "Well," the old cowboy answered, "I guess it's because I ain't enough of a 'sportsman.' We don't shoot any game out here unless we need meat or want a change from beef, and we seldom want a change from beef."

"Then why did you take a gun with you?"

"Oh, just because I sort of like to once in a while. I might see a mountain lion or a wolf and take a chance shot at 'em, or I might run acrost some human wolf that I'd want to smoke out of the country."

"What about bears?" Scootie asked. "They're bad too, and they eat people."

"No, Scootie, they have better taste than that. They eat berries, ants, fish, honey and such like."

"How do they catch fish?"

"Slap 'em out of the water onto the bank with a front paw."

With day after day of such goings on to interest the kids, while on horseback most of the time, they natural-like fell into riding without hardly realizing it. Sometimes the old cowboy would move some little bunch

"What about bears?"

WILL JAMES

of cattle from one part of the range to the other, or a bunch of horses would be brought in and corralled, and in their excitement to help with whatever Uncle Bill did there come a time when they put their horses to a lope or a trot as natural and without thinking as sticking a potato with a fork. Of course they wasn't nowheres near what's called good riders as yet, for it takes more than a few days or a few months' practice and experience to be classed as what's called a good rider in the West. But they'd got to where they wasn't so conscious of their riding, and that was a mighty good start. All they'd need now would be more days in the saddle, and work while sitting there, like chasing cattle or horses over rough country, not just plain riding.

They had a good chance at the kind of riding that makes a rider a rider, for Uncle Bill never cared to ride just to be riding. That struck him about as interesting as it would the kids going to school when school was out. The old cowboy wanted some reason for saddling up a horse and going out riding, some work, and while going out with the kids most every day he was keeping an eye on the stock, moving a bunch now and again or hunting up some that was missing. That all was more interesting to the kids too, and teached 'em a lot of things they'd never got to learn by just plain riding around.

Then, to make things even better and more interesting than they'd been, Uncle Frank rode in with his cowboys one evening and breaks the news that the neighboring outfits had "pooled" together for round-up and branding, and that the whole spread of round-up wagons and riders was headed for the Five-Barb range, when Uncle Frank and his own riders would join the outfit and ride with 'em from there on for a spell. Of course, Kip and Scootie and Uncle Bill could come along too.

It was hard to tell which of the three was the happiest at the news. The kids had a hunch from the talks they heard that the goings-on would be a heap interesting, maybe as interesting as a circus, but Uncle Bill couldn't and didn't try to compare being with a round-up spread with anything else. If he had it'd been nothing short of going to heaven a-horseback. For being on round-up, gathering, joking and riding with old friends was something that every cowboy looks forward to with a heap of pleasure, even if there is a heap of work. The cowboy rides steady and on an average of eighteen hours a day during round-up, but the gathering of so many riders makes the work that much more interesting and plenty full of happenings.

It didn't take the Five-Barb cowboys long to gather what saddle horses was needed, for most of 'em ranged pretty close to the ranch. While that was being done, Uncle Bill picked out one of the ranch hands, told him to get a good team and wagon together and be ready to drive it soon as the riders got back, rolled their beds and loaded 'em in. Then he went to the commissary and dug up a little tent which was also to go in the wagon. That tent was to be used as Scootie's private bedroom while on round-up. As for Kip, he was going to sleep in a regular tarpaulin-covered bed when night come, like all the cowboys did, and with the whole sky for a roof.

The kids done a lot of running around following busy Uncle Bill. They didn't have time to ask many questions but they sort of made up for that by watching. Tall dusts begin to appear from many places in the valley. The cowboys had rode away from the ranch before daybreak, and it was only about middle forenoon now and they was already coming back with many horses. Bunch after bunch was corralled, and after the big gate closed on the last bunch there come the work of cutting out the horses that wasn't wanted. Them was run into another corral.

After that was done there was fresh horses caught and saddled, an early noon bait was fast swallowed down by all hands, Kip and Scootie too, and in a few minutes all was back to the corrals again, horses was mounted and "topped off," corral gates was opened and soon the whole outfit of riders, saddle horses and wagon lined out to join the round-up spread. Kip's and Scootie's spirit was a-soaring sky high. They was in the lead and riding between two uncles, Frank and Bill.

The line of the Five-Barb range was reached that afternoon. The outfit went on, over a couple of low summits and it was near sundown when, riding down into a big valley, Uncle Frank pointed to where the round-up spread was camped. It was a couple of miles away, and on account of a long line of trees the kids couldn't see the camp, but they seen what looked like cattle. Only, they thought, that dark circle in the valley couldn't be cattle, there couldn't be that many cattle in the world. To one side, and more scattered was what looked like more stock and as they rode on they seen that them was all horses. What a bunch of 'em there was! Kip guessed there was about a thousand. Scootie guessed there was more than that, and when they asked Uncle Bill they was surprised when he said there was only about two hundred.

The bellering of cattle came to their ears. They didn't know what it was at first. In the quiet of the evening it sounded like steady low rumbling of far away thunder, and then they seen that the big dark circle was sure enough cattle. They could now make out the shape of 'em and the riders that was holding the big herd close together. For it was time to get 'em on "Bed-ground" where all cowboys would take turn holding 'em for the night, on night guard.

That all was a great sight for the kids, a sight they'd never dreamed could be seen on earth. Then the big fire of the camp come to sight, it'd been hid by the big cottonwoods along the creek, and there they seen many riders, some stretched flat to the ground and the others standing or squatted around the fire.

All looked towards the Five-Barb outfit as it rambled in, and many came to the rope corral as the horses was run in and the riders unsaddled. There was many different greetings heard as all met, such as "Why, if it ain't the old so-and-so himself, hair and hide," or "Hello, you old reprobate, thought I left you for hung last time I seen you," and such like. The kids was unsaddling their own horses and had some laughs at the remarks. They'd been plum overlooked, till some of the remarks got to be too much for men's ears only, and then Uncle Bill let out a warning holler.

"Hold on, cowboys," he says, "I forgot to tell you there's a lady in our outfit." He called Scootie, and introducing her to the bunch of grinning riders he went on to tell her: "You got to excuse these knee-sprung buzzards for their talk. They all wear number four hats, and all they know is how to ride a horse and turn a cow. Do not heareth what they sayeth."

Scootie laughed. "I didn't hear 'em say very bad words," she says, "I heard a lot worse ones at school."

"So did I," says Kip, who'd just showed himself. "And I know quite a few worse ones."

There was no more introducing needed, the kids had introduced themselves well and now they was escorted to the chuck wagon where, on the chuck-box apron, was tin plates, cups, utensils and seasonings. One of the riders proceeded to wait on Scootie, and with a dish towel over one arm he tried to imitate some highfaluting waiter in both action and words as he made the rounds of the big iron kettles and ovens and filling her plate of whatever she might want. Kip followed close, and then came Uncle Bill and the other riders.

The kids was hungry. Their plates and cups was filled, and as they squatted down on the sod to eat, holding the plates in their laps like all the cowboys did, they didn't remember of a time when they enjoyed a meal more, not even the Thanksgiving turkey dinners, and while eating and listening to the talk amongst the many riders that was gathered around, the light of fire playing on 'em, darkness outside the circle, stars above, the night air, jingling of spurs, sounds of hoofs and far away bellering of cattle, that all made a combination they'd always remember even if they seen a thousand more such gatherings.

The meal was over, the talk went on, old happenings was brought back to memory and new ones was discussed, and many good stories was told. Then one rider and another got up and walked away, two and then three, till most all had hit for their bedgrounds of tarps covered "soogans" (quilts). Uncle Frank stirred the kids out of their trance and told 'em they'd better hit for their soogans too, that morning comes awful fast at a round-up camp.

It wasn't very many minutes later when the "hoot" of a night owl was heard, but only the men on guard and the "nighthawk"* heard it, for all the other riders was now riding in slumberland. Only one spot showed in the dark of the night, that was Scootie's tent.

*Night horse wrangler.

CHAPTER TEN

IT WAS LESS THAN three hours after midnight when the "flunky" (cook's helper) was stirred out of his soogans by one of the riders coming off nightguard shift. The flunky built a fire at the pot rack and then the cook got up and went to work. The meat had already been cut the night before, the potatoes had been peeled, the biscuits flour mixed and the coffee ground, and half an hour after the cook put on his flour-sack apron he let out his early morning holler to "come and get it." It was still dark when the riders slipped into their boots, washed and ambled to the fire, and there was only a faint sign of daybreak when the "remuda" (saddle horses) was brought in the rope corral and breakfast was over with. By sun-up they was quite a few miles from camp and not so far from a point where they would scatter and circle back towards camp, combing the range of all cattle they found before the heat of the day made 'em hide in the shade of the brush.

Kip and Scootie didn't hear the cook's holler on their first morning at the round-up camp, nor did they hear the riders saddle up and ride away. Kip was the first to wake up, and that was on account of the heat of the sun that begin beating down on him and a few flies buzzing around and lighting on his nose and ears. When he straightened up in his bed the camp looked pretty deserted, not a horse was in sight and he couldn't even see the cook nor flunky. Them two and the nighthawk was stretched out in the shade of the chuck-wagon and taking a short snooze while the taking was good.

Kip jumped up and dressed in a hurry, sort of half scared that he was left alone in the big camp. Then he seen Scootie's tent. He throwed a handful of small pebbles at it and when his sister's surprised holler was heard he felt better, for he wasn't quite alone.

Scootie's holler woke up the cook and by the time they washed up and came to the chuck wagon he had things warmed up ready for 'em.

"Where are all the cowboys and Uncle Frank and Uncle Bill?" Kip asks the cook, as him and Scootie was sitting on a bed roll and eating their breakfast of fried beef, potatoes and biscuits.

"They all been gone a long time, but they'll be back with a herd in a couple of hours now. They'll be making a long ride, and both the uncles told me to tell you kids to stay close to camp till they get back, then you'll get your horses and watch the branding."

That seemed to please 'em plenty enough, and after they had their breakfast they went to scouting around camp and do some close exploring. About thirty tarp-

They'll be making a long ride.

covered beds was scattered around the camp, some was left laying flat, others was rolled and a few was wide open for airing. Cowboy belongings was by every bed and the kids noticed that a few was so rich as to own an extra pair of boots. (This was a northern outfit and where the foremen allowed their riders to take their own beds and some belongings. There was no "doubling up" and wagons was furnished a plenty to carry the beds from camp to camp.)

The kids missed Uncle Bill as they went investigating around and exploring, not only because of questions they might want to ask him but also for his company. They'd got so used to his shadow being alongside of theirs, and wether he was answering their questions or just talking, the world opened up to 'em a heap more when he was near.

The old cowboy didn't figure they'd miss him. If anything he thought they'd be glad to be away from him for a change and not being told what and what not to do. Besides, he sort of wanted to visit with the cowboys he'd knowed for so long. Then the freer life of round-up time was in his blood and he was living again as he lived many years past. He was having his vacation from the ranch the same as the kids was having theirs from the city.

The kids went on exploring. They zigzagged from one bed to another, fingering different strange things they seen, looked into the wagons, walked on up the creek a ways, and they was turning back when a rider caught up with 'em. He was a young feller, not so many years older than Kip and the kids recognized him as the boy who'd took the horses out of the rope corral the evening before. He was the day horse wrangler.

The wrangler stopped his horse and grinned down at the kids, specially at Scootie, who wasn't at all hard to look at.

He was the day horse wrangler.

"Some of the 'Drives' (herds) are beginning to come in pretty fast," he says, "and I'm riding in to tell 'Cookie.' . . . If you kids want to see the drives, climb up on the point of that ridge."

He pointed out the ridge, it was close to camp, and he rode on, leaving 'em wondering what he meant by drives and cookie. They would ask Uncle Bill.

But they got a fair hunch of what he meant by drives soon as they got on the point of the ridge. From there they seen half a dozen high-soaring dusts and stirring each dust was many cattle. The bunches was drove sort of fan-shape, each bunch brought closer to the other as they neared camp. Then, while still a couple of miles away one bunch after another was throwed in with the center bunch till all formed one big herd. The herd was checked up and held when within a quarter of a mile from camp, a few riders was left to hold 'em there and

all the others strung out on a high lope the rest of the
way on in to camp for a noon bait and a change to fresh
horses which the wrangler was now bringing in.

The kids run down to the corral but the riders
beat 'em there, and Uncle Bill was already unsaddling
when they come near.

"Well, you sleepy heads," says the old cowboy, as
he sees 'em, "who got you out of bed?"

"The flies did," says Kip, grinning.

"And Kip got me up," says Scootie. "He threw rocks
at my tent."

"It wasn't rocks, only little pebbles."

"Well, they sounded like big rocks, and they scared
me."

The kids followed Uncle Bill wherever he went like
they was afraid he might vanish any second, and noticing that gave the old cowboy a sort of queer feeling
that went from the pit of his stomach on up to his Adam's
apple. "The little rascals did miss me," he thought to
himself.

Uncle Frank joined 'em for the noon meal, but there
wasn't much time spent on that meal, no long conver-
sation or any such thing, and soon the empty plates
was heard drop in the "round-up pan"* and the cowboys rolled their cigarettes while on their way to the
corrals to catch fresh horses. The kids couldn't figure
out how they could eat in such little time, but, as a rule,
a cowboy is not a very heavy eater.

* Dish pan.

Uncle Frank caught Scootie's horse and Uncle Bill caught Kip's, and by the time all got to where the herd was being held, a fire had been started a little ways from the herd, and while the many branding irons was heating a few ropers, mostly "reps,"* looked the herd over to sort of spot what belonged to their outfit. A ring of about fifteen riders was around the herd to keep the cattle from breaking out or scattering, and no more milling was done than could be helped on account the calves might get separated from their mammies. Each calf had to be with its mother before it was roped and branded so it could be identified as to what outfit it belonged to. There was the brands of many outfits in that herd and the ropers had to be careful to read the "iron" (brand) the cow packed before the calf that followed her was roped and branded.

Uncle Bill stopped his horse not far from the branding fire and where the kids would have a good chance

* Riders representing the outfit they worked for.

Each calf had to be with its mother before it was roped.

to watch the roping and branding. Scootie was on one side of him and Kip on the other. A freckle-faced, red-headed cowboy rode by and, hinting at the old cowboy, started to imitate the sound of a cackling old hen with her chicks.

"Kut kut kut kut kut kutut kut kutut kutut kutut kutut . . ."

"Get in the herd and hide, you flea bitten stag," grins Uncle Bill, "or somebody might take pity on you and shoot you."

There was a calf's surprised and scared beller, and the kids looked in time to see a loop draw up on both its hind legs. The calf tried to buck and pull away but he couldn't do much and soon was drug the little ways to the fire where two wrasslers grabbed him. One jerked on the tight rope while the other reached over the bucking calf's wither, got hold of one front leg with the right hand and the flank with the left and turned him over to come down flat on his side. Hanging on the front leg, the first wrassler held him down with one knee on the neck and the other on the shoulder. The other wrassler then grabbed the upper hind leg, took the rope off so the roper could go on and get another calf while this one was being branded, then stuck his foot above the hock of the lower hind leg and held the calf well stretched out that way. Of course the calf didn't agree to any of that and it done a heap of bellering and bucking and kicking in the short time before he was layed flat.

There was two sets of wrasslers and three ropers and the calves was being branded at the rate of one a minute. Different outfits have different ways of working while branding. Some use two ropers to each calf. One ropes it by the neck and the other by the hind feet, one wrassler turns the calf over, branding side up, and the two ropers keep it stretched.

Kip and Scootie didn't get to watch everything as the first calf was brought in, earmarked and branded. There was too much going on all at once and they didn't have time to ask any questions for a spell. But as calf after calf, big and little, was brought in and all bellered and bucked, Scootie finally managed to pass a remark.

"Goodness, Uncle Bill," she says, "that branding certainly must hurt them."

"Well," says the old cowboy, "I don't guess it feels very good, but they're more scared than hurt. It's over in less than a minute anyway and I don't think it hurts any worse than having a tooth pulled."

"But what about afterwards, doesn't the burn keep on hurting?"

"I guess it does, a little, but they sure don't seem to lose any sleep or fat over it."

That seemed to satisfy her some, and she went on watching and smelling of the smoke of the burning hair. Then Kip asked, "What do they cut pieces off their ears for?"

"That's what we call earmarking. And so we can tell from a long ways whose cattle they are without having to ride close and look at the brand, or if you're on the wrong side of the critter and can't see the brand, she'll look at you, her ears come forward and you can identify her by the way her ears are cut, like if you wore a white shirt and Scootie wore a red one I could tell from a long ways which one of you was which."

"But," says Scootie, "does all that have to be done to them so they can be recognized?"

"Yep. You see, Scootie, these cattle are running free on the range, and not in pastures. They drift quite a bit while hunting for the best of feed, shade, and water and shelter. During a bad winter storm they sometimes drift with it, and if the storm keeps up for days they'll drift till they find good shelter amongst trees or in deep canyons. Range cattle have drifted as far as fifty miles from their home range in one storm and strayed on other ranges where nobody would know who they belonged to, if it wasn't for the brands and earmarks on 'em. Even the owner of 'em wouldn't know them without the brands, for he don't see some of the cattle over once or twice a year and if he did recognize a few of the 'markers' he'd have a hard time to prove that them markers and the bunch with 'em was his unless he had a mighty fine lot of witnesses to help him. You can easy enough get witnesses if you only have a little dairy herds that's kept in a pasture and where the farm

Ropers kept a bringing calves one right after another and steady.

hands see 'em every day, but when it comes to having four or five thousand head of cattle like your Uncle Frank has, cattle that's running loose and mixing with others of the same breed and owned by other cattlemen, I think it'd take more than wizards to tell whose is whose, and there'd be many an argument. Not only that, but the cattle rustler would sure have a picnic. He'd soon stick his brand on 'em and he'd have as easy a time accumulating a herd as a kid would have picking up candy after they leaked out thru a hole in your pocket. Supposing the kid had a sack of the same kind of candy you had you'd have a hard time identifying your own, wouldn't you? . . . It'd be just as hard with a big bunch of cattle, like in this herd for instance."

"But isn't there some other way of marking the cattle without having to brand them?"

"None that would stick and couldn't easy be changed, and even some of the brands have been disfigured and changed by rustlers, often."

Ropers kept a-bringing calves one right after another and steady, and as Scootie watched she sort of got used to seeing the hot irons sear the slick hides. Everything was done so quick and smooth, and it seemed like a calf was no more than brought in when it was turned loose again, free to go back to its mammy and packing the same brand she wore.

Kip didn't have nothing to say about the goings on, he was too busy watching and he only wished he could be with the wrasslers and help. Uncle Bill would of liked to been in the herd and roping, but he liked to be with the kids too and he wanted to make up with 'em for leaving 'em that morning. As he talked, he kept a little book and pencil in his hands and as each roper brought in a calf to be branded hollered out the brand its mother packed, the calf was branded the same, and Uncle Bill added a mark in his tally book along the brand he'd drawed there. That was to keep track of how many cattle belonged to each owner, male and female.

There was many brands in the little tally book, and as Kip got to glancing at it once in a while he wondered what the names of 'em was. Finally he had to ask.

"There's thousands of different kinds of brands," says the old cowboy, as he started to explain. "The most of 'em are easy enough to read, and in reading 'em you always start from the top and left, like with this one for instance." He showed him the tally book. "That reads $\overline{2U}$ 'Bar two U' this one 'M seven bar' $\underline{M7}$ and so on. Straight letters or figure brands like them are easy to read, but any cowboy is liable to give some brands a different name if it's a 'character' brand and he's never heard of it before, like with

$\times$ 'walking X' that's a letter and character brand mixed and a stranger cowboy could just as well call it Double L, or the 'Long X,' $\times$ Double Y,

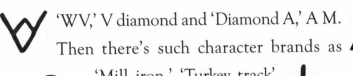

'WV,' V diamond and 'Diamond A,' A M. Then there's such character brands as 'Mill iron,' 'Turkey track' and the like. You got to pretty well hear them named before you can be sure of 'em.

He drawed out many different brands which was used in scattered and far away parts of the cow country and gave Kip and Scootie quite a bit of education in brand reading. Scootie thought that some of the brands made pretty nice designs while Kip wondered which one he'd like to use best when he got a herd of his own some day.

That day's branding was near over, the last few calves got their life's marking. The fire was put out and then begin the work of cutting out the cattle that belonged on that range. Then is when the kids got to see some mighty fine action of cowhorses at work. No steer or cow or calf likes to be singled out of a herd, it's their nature to stick together for protection, and when a rider singles one to be drove out, that one does a heap of fast dodging trying to stay in or get back. It takes a quick

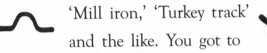

WILLJAMES '30

horse and a good rider and both have to savvy the game well to do the work.

Some horses was so good at the work that they could tell the second a rein touched their necks which critter their riders had spotted to be cut out, and from then on they'd manouver by dodges and turns to get that critter out without hardly any more feel of the reins. Man and horse worked together the same as if the two was one.

With the big herd, the action going on in and around it, the tall dust soaring a mile high, the sun slanting on horns, hides and leather, the spreading of big country surrounded by tall mountains and far away blue ridges, all that to see while sitting on two good horses was as fine a sight as Kip and Scootie could ever wish for, they could of well used an extra pair of eyes so as they could of took in everything.

All the cattle belonging to that range was cut out and let go. Then the ones that was kept, which was all strays and belonging to other ranges, was drove to the other herd of strays which had been gathered during round-ups of the days before. More strays would be found as the round-up outfit moved on, and as different ranges was rode thru, them strays would be cut out and left where they belonged. The calves would be all branded and they'd be free to roam again till next round-up time, along in the fall. In some range countries the round-up outfits are out and working the year around, taking

Seldom knowing or caring what month of the year it might be.

'em five or six months to cover their range, and by the time they make the circle and get back to one point it's time to go on and cover it over again, because by that time there's more calves to brand, more cattle to move and shipping of beef to be done. Sundays, Thanksgivings, Christmases and all kinds of holidays come and go as just another day and the cowboy rides on just the same, seldom knowing or caring what month of the year it might be.

CHAPTER ELEVEN

U NCLE FRANK AND HIS RIDERS had been
with the round-up outfit for over a week, and so
had Kip and Scootie and Uncle Bill. There'd been a
lot of country covered in that time, the outfit had moved
camp every day or so and new camps was made in new
countries always, sometimes in timbered hills and
mountains, other times in broken, rolling, or prairie grass
lands, then cut-up badlands of many colors where cattle
was hard to gather.

The kids kept a-looking, seeing, hearing and learning.
A few times, Uncle Bill took 'em with him on "inside
circle,"* and twice he took 'em where the herd was held
for the night and gave 'em a taste of nightguard. They
liked that, the nights was nice, the cattle was quiet and
all seemed mighty peaceful. And it was, but the old cowboy
told 'em of many times when things wasn't that way, when
lightning played close, cloudbursts come and big herds
stampeded away, when horses fell, riders was hurt and
cattle scattered to all points of the earth. Other times
when cold and wet snow would be falling, cold winds
blowing, herd restless and cowboys about freezing on their
horses. The kids couldn't get no idea of such goings on.

*Shortest of round-up ride.

They could only try to use their imagination, and they done their best at that. Kip had looked up at the starry sky hoping to see a thunder cloud come. He'd like to seen a stampede.

They rode around and around the bedded herd as the old cowboy talked, passed riders making the same rounds, only in opposite directions. They looked only a little darker than the night and was hard to see, so was the herd.

"Sometimes," Uncle Bill had said, "a herd is stampeded by a cowboy just lighting a cigarette, the sudden flare of the match will do it."

Kip's hopes of seeing a stampede sort of shot up at that. He looked for it whenever the old cowboy rolled a cigarette and lit it, but he was disappointed every time, for the cigarette was never lit close to the herd and the match being held in close-cupped hands never showed a flare.

"I haven't seen a cowboy smoke a pipe," Kip said, still thinking of flaring matches. "Don't they smoke anything but cigarettes?"

"Not hardly. A cowboy can't very well pack anything that's apt to break, like a pipe. He'd have to keep a supply of 'em in his bed roll and even then they're apt to get broke. That's why the tobacco that comes in a sack is best for us. That can't be hurt if a horse falls on it, and after getting the wrinkles out of a cigarette paper a good smoke can always be rolled."

Then Scootie had spoke up. "Can you roll a cigarette in one hand?" she'd asked. "The cowboys in the
movies do it."

"No," Uncle Bill grinned, "I can't do that, but I guess
anybody could learn to if they tried and had plenty of
time, but while I got my two hands I might just as well
be using 'em."

There was times when the horse wrangler sort of
relieved the old cowboy in answering questions, keeping
company and watching over the kids. A couple of mornings
they'd rode with him and followed him as he herded the
remuda out to graze, and that young feller felt mighty
glad, and much bigger and older in their company. His
talk and actions was more like a grown man's instead
of just a kid of sixteen, and he wasn't acting or putting
on in any way. It was on account that he'd been brought
up amongst grown folks and seldom had a chance to mix
with kids of his age only when he went to school, and
that'd only been for a few winters. The rest of the time,
and from a baby on up he'd heard no younger talk than
his dad's and mother's. He was six months old when he
seen and blinked at his first round-up, and he begin joking
with the cowboys before he could manouver his tongue.
His dad was range boss of the pool outfit and now it
looked like such a responsible job would be his in a very
few years. He savvied cattle and horses, range and riders
and some of the remarks he'd pass would sort of remind
the kids of Uncle Bill.

But with all his wise ways and old-timer talk, his heart was all kid and his laugh always ready, his slim and wiry body always on trigger edge for action, in fun or in work, riding bucking horses or handling a herd.

While him and the kids watched the remuda he explained the wrangler job to 'em, how his work started in the morning and soon as the night wrangler brought the horses in the rope corral. The rope corral used on round-ups, and only for horses, is made up of a heavy rope cable which stretched in a tight circle and held up

The rope corral used on round-ups and only for horses.

about three feet off the ground by forked sticks. In moving camp the cable is coiled up and stretched again at the next one. Soon as the cowboys have caught their horses the others are let out of the corral to graze on some more, and as the young feller says, they're not run out or jammed around in any rush, but just sort of pointed one way and left to scatter and graze and water and free to rest. A count is made on 'em and they have to be watched pretty close because scattered out the way they are some will try to get away. Many are wise to the wrangler, they'll act plum innocent, graze slow till they get out of his sight, behind a knoll or amongst some trees, and then start out on a long trot for wherever their home range is.

The remuda is seldom crowded into a trot when being corralled and a good wrangler will see that the horses are not kept in the corral any longer than possible and that they'll get every chance there is to good grass, water and shade.

When the horses are still and resting and don't need much watching, he uses that time to gather some dry wood for the cook, for that's also the wrangler's job, and it's all to how good wood he gets or how cranky the cook is wether he'll have a bite of anything special which some cooks sometimes make and put away. Wood is sometimes hard to get and few wranglers do any tree chopping if they can help it. They'll gather loose dry limbs, put their loop around the pile, take a couple of turns around the saddle horn with the rope and drag the wood in a-horseback. Everything is done on horseback and with a rope, if possible.

The young feller liked to rope, and as him and the kids rode watch on the remuda he spread loop after loop over bushes and rocks or anything for a loop to go around. He was a good roper, for he'd had a rope in his hands pretty well ever since he could pack one.

One time Scootie asked him to try and rope her. He grinned and shook his head, remarking that it's a poor stunt to try and rope anybody because the loop might land pretty hard sometimes and when the rope is drawed it might make burns along the neck or arms.

"I seen a feller knock a horse's eye out with a rope one time," he says. "Of course he didn't mean to, but he had one of these heavy brass hondoos that you see on ropes once in a while. No cowboy ever uses them, and when he threwed his loop the hondoo hit the horse right in the eye."

Scootie didn't ask to be roped any more after hearing that, and from then on when her and Kip played with ropes and tried to catch one another they only roped at one another's feet, good enough practice, as half the roping on the range is to the feet of both cattle and horses, "front-footing" and "heeling," and that's harder to do than to catch by the head or horns.

Either with the young wrangler, or Uncle Bill, sometimes with busy Uncle Frank or some other cowboy the kids got to see and understand pretty well what all went on around a round-up outfit. Of course they didn't get to pitch in and do any work because they was too little and inexperienced to do anything as yet, and it was figured that it would be best and a heap safer to just stay on their horses and watch. They did that well, and there was only one time when Kip sort of "forgot."

He was close to the herd one day, watching the cutting out of some cattle when a yearling broke out of the herd close to him and hit for open country. Kip's wise old horse, as was natural when a cowboy was on him, made a quick move after the yearling and the first thing Kip knowed he was right agreeing with the horse in heading off that yearling and bringing it back. If he'd knowed of the speed he'd have to ride to head off the yearling he might not of started after it, but he wasn't caring about that now, and giving his horse a little free rein, that horse done the work of cutting the distance down to that yearling. Kip had never rode half so fast since he'd been at the ranch and he was having a little trouble keeping his breath.

Uncle Bill was right close when Kip started after the yearling. At first he was for hollering at him to let the yearling go, but he didn't, and now as he watched the kid's fast running horse he wished he had, for Kip was riding a pretty fair cow horse and quick on the turn. The old cowboy jumped his horse and raced in after him, holding his breath as he seen that Kip's horse had caught up with the yearling and, of his own accord, was going to turn it. Kip was just hanging on.

Then come a jolt and a sudden turn, Kip's hands was jerked loose from what all he grabbed a hold of and was sent a-sailing to a hard landing. But he'd no more than landed when he bounced up like a rubber ball. His horse had stopped still, and without brushing the dirt off himself or looking around only where the yearling had went, he jumped on his horse and rode after it again.

Then come a jolt
and a sudden turn.

Uncle Bill took a long breath and grinned as he watched him. "That kid's got the 'makings,' " he'd said to himself.

The heifer was headed off a second time, and Kip come mighty near falling off a second time too, but not quite. He was still a foot or so off the ground when his horse stopped, and when he pulled himself up in the saddle the heifer had dodged past once more and was quite a ways from the herd now. Kip thought then that he might just as well let it go on that account, but Uncle Bill rode up about then and told him, acting severe, to get the yearling back, that a cowboy never lets anything get away.

Kip would sure remember that. He let his horse go after the yearling, and this time with a mind set to bring it back. Of course the horse would do the manouvering of bringing it back because Kip had more than his hands full doing nothing else but trying to stay on him, and finally, after a few turnings and dodgings, and Kip hanging on to everything, the yearling was headed back for the herd.

He was a little proud when that was done, but soon as he got close to Uncle Bill and Scootie that was soon took out of him, and by none other than his sister who was laughing till tears had come to her eyes.

"You looked so funny going over your horse's head," she said, between laughs, "just like a big leap frog jumping off a creek bank."

Kip got red in the face and glanced at the old cowboy who was trying hard to keep a straight face, and then he came back at Scootie.

"If you'd been riding that horse you couldn't have done any better."

Scootie laughed some more. "I should say not," she said. "I could never leap that well."

Scootie had the last word, and more than that, for she added on that he'd grabbed the saddle horn and everything he could get a hold of every time the horse turned, after Uncle Bill telling him that he should never do that.

Kip had nothing to say to that, it was sure enough true. But that didn't worry him so much as the fall he'd took. Scootie would never forget that and would tell of it every chance she could, she more than enjoyed having some such things to tell on him and he knowed from past experience that she could make a good story and so everybody would have a good laugh on him. He sort of pictured his dad and mother smiling about it when they'd be told, and then all the kids in school pointing a finger and laughing at him as being "a cowboy that can't ride a horse."

There'd be only one way of having Scootie keep quiet and that'd be if the same thing happened to her, or some other happening that she wouldn't want Kip to tell of about her.

But their last night at the round-up outfit come and nothing happened that would bring a laugh on Scootie.

But there was time yet, and Kip hoped and near prayed that something with the makings of a good joke to tell on her would happen. One day something finally did, and so far above what all he'd hoped that he was willing to have Scootie tell on him so he could feel free to go ahead and tell on her.

That happening come a month or so after they'd come back to the ranch from the round-up. The kids had got pretty wise to things by then and Uncle Bill wasn't keeping as close a watch on 'em as he had. Some days he'd just catch their horses for 'em, ride away and leave 'em by themselves and to do as they wished for a whole half a day at a time. Sometimes they rode and other times they just fooled around the ranch.

They was playing around the ranch one day, afoot, and going from one building and corral to another. Both had their ropes with 'em and was sort of practicing at catching different things as they went. Then they come to the calf pen. A few gentle, but good feeling milk cow's calves was kept inside it and the sight of 'em sort of invited the kids at good rope practice. They'd practiced roping at 'em before but always when Uncle Bill was around. This time they was alone and they got more reckless in their roping and playing.

There'd been a heavy shower the day before, the calf pen was a little muddy and in a low place was a pool of sticky black mud. The kids stayed on the dryest ground they could and started roping. They was getting pretty good with a rope and was now getting so they could catch a calf by the neck once in every five throws or so. The calves, being gentle, could easy enough be walked up to after each catch and the rope took off.

The roping went on for a spell, and when they got a little tired of that they got to wondering of what else to do, and that's how come they thought of riding the calves after roping 'em. Kip caught one little feller, got on it and had the time of his life staying on as the calf bucked around the corral a little. That was a lot of fun. Scootie roped and rode one too, and then she caught

They was getting pretty good with a rope.

the second calf before Kip did his. This second calf was a little bigger and not so gentle as the others, and as Kip watched her climb on him he sort of warned her that she'd have to do some hard riding on that one.

And she did have to do some hard riding, but it didn't last long, just long enough for the calf to buck and run acrost the corral to the pool of mud. It looked like the calf had figured on that muddy hole, maybe to teach the kids a lesson to leave him alone. Anyway he bucked in straight line till he come to that pool and, quick as a flash, he made another buck-jump right by the side of it, turned and sent Scootie scooting her whole length into the pool.

Kip about choked laughing seeing her splash in the pool and then seeing her scramble out of it on all fours. She was green-black mud from head to foot and couldn't of been better covered with it if she'd wallered in the pool a-purpose.

She made quite a sight as she came out of the pool and stood up and started to wipe her face with her muddy hands, and maybe she'd laughed at the happening too, but Kip was doing plenty enough of that for two, and soon as she got the mud out of her eyes so she could see a little and seen him doubled up in his laughing fit, she got a little peeved and made him do his laughing while on the run, for she took after him and done her best to catch him and give him a taste of a splash in the muddy hole.

But Kip wasn't weighted down with no mud and he kept out of her reach easy enough. So giving up catching him she went to the creek to wash up as best she could and then to the house where Martha gave her a good bath and a whole change of clothes, even to boots, for them was filled with mud too.

She was all cleaned up and like nothing unusual happened when Uncle Bill rode back to the ranch that day, and she was surprised at what a nice brother she had when he didn't tell the old cowboy of the happening. But she had a strong hunch why he didn't tell, that it was so she would never tell about him falling off his horse. There was no word understanding about that but none was needed, she would never tell on Kip now for fear he would tell on her, and Kip acted like he *might* be trusted not to tell.

CHAPTER TWELVE

I T WAS GETTING ALONG late summer, three of Frank's cowboys was scattered at different camps on his range, "riding line" to sort of keep strays from drifting in and the Five-Barb stock from drifting out, also to once in a while brand some of the calves that'd been missed in the round-up. The rough-string rider had run in some range horses, picked a string of likely geldings out of the bunches and was breaking 'em and getting 'em ready to do a little fall work. Two other riders caught their private horses, tied their beds and belongings on the extra ones and rode away for other ranges. The cutting and stacking of the wild hay was in full swing and they could of took on that job if they wanted to, or they could of stayed at the ranch without any charges till they could go to riding again during fall round-

"Riding line."

up, but them two riders wasn't interested in haying or any work where a man is afoot. Theirs was while on a horse. They'd rode on to look for that kind of work, and if they didn't get too far away they'd be back again when fall works started.

Outside of Uncle Frank and Uncle Bill there was only one cowboy on the ranch, and that was the feller breaking the horses. The hay hands had took the place of riders for a couple of months. They done the work of stacking up feed for the winter so that the weakest and oldest stock could be pulled thru. The Five-Barb seldom had to feed over twenty five percent of the cattle during winters and then for only about two months.

With the cutting and stacking of hay there was something else new for Kip and Scootie to watch and see done. They rode on hay wagons, climbed haystacks and had a lot of fun, but there was nothing they could do in that work, excepting to get in the way. Another thing everything was pretty well the same every day, there was no new country to see and they couldn't chase anything in a hay wagon.

So, after a while in the big hay fields, they went back to their horses and rode with Uncle Bill again. Or else they'd be down by the corrals and watching the rider at his work of gentling and breaking the big spooky horses. That was interesting to them. No two horses acted alike and each showed a variety of action that made the watching always new.

They liked it best when one of the broncs would buck, not only for the riding and the bucking but also for the way the rider played his long "tapideros."* He'd play them over rump and shoulder of a bucking horse and make them pop like a shot out of a gun, sometimes scaring a horse right out of his bucking spell.

"Tapideros are good for many other things besides helping gentle a bronc," says the rider one time, after the kids asked him what they was for. "They're good while working a herd and cutting out cattle. You can just pop 'em a little and a critter will hit out like a can was tied to her tail. Then in the summer they keep the hot sun from beating down on your feet, and in the winter they shelter them from cold winds and snows."

The kids watched him ride a green bronc out of the corral one day. The horse had only been rode a couple of times and wasn't as yet bridlewise. He was stiff-necked and hard to turn, and when just a little ways from the corral he broke into a fit of bucking and stampeding. Then is when the kids seen another good use for the long taps'. The horse was heading for a high straight bank where the land dropped twenty feet or more. There was no turning the horse by pulling on the rein and, so, the rider brought his taps' to work. He rapped the horse's ears with 'em and then popped 'em alongside of his head and nose, soon enough and as one tap' kept a-popping him on one side of the face the horse begin to turn and head the other way. If it hadn't been for

*Leather covering which fits over the stirrups and hangs down underneath.

them taps' the spooky would of most likely bucked down over the bank.

With happenings of one kind and another going on that way, while at the ranch, in the big pastures and fields or while on the range, the kids went right on with their learning of the ways and works of the range country. They was fast getting familiar with so many things that had puzzled 'em at first, and they got to wondering how they come to ask all the questions they did. As day after day went by they got to

As one tap' kept a-popping him on one side of the face the horse begun to turn.

asking less and less questions, being they understood things some, could do more, and was more able to take care of themselves and they could enjoy everything a heap better.

If they did ask questions now they was more of a general kind, like Kip asked Uncle Bill one day:

"How long does it take to learn to be a good cowboy?"

"That's kind of hard to answer," Uncle Bill had said. "To be a good cowboy depends first on the man and on his nerve, spirit and natural ability, then how young he starts, what kind of countries and outfits he works in and for, how steady he works, what kind of horses he hires out to ride, and so on. Then there's many stages and many things to learn in the cowboy game, as much as there is in any profession or business. Some get to the top as cattle owners, build towns where there was only a stock yard, own a bank or two, and I know a few of the forty dollar a month riders who rode on to be governors of their state and made camp in that office.

"But like with any other game, there's men on the range who are happy to be just cowboys, not accumulate too much to worry about, and with their few horses and their experience they're as independent as the man they're riding for, and more free.

"The cowboy's life is a whole lot fitting for a young feller. It gets him down to earth, stirs up a spirit in him that makes him want to be good at the game without any thought at the hard way of living and low wages.

With a few horses and their experience they're as independent as the man they're riding for, and more free.

There's first hand learning that makes him self-reliant and which stirs up a heap of confidence, and is a teaching which all goes a mighty long ways in any other game he might want to tackle later on.

"There's a heap more to being a good cowboy than just knowing how to ride and throw a rope, and if you was to ask me how much I know about the game I could easy tell you that I'm just beginning to learn, for you see I've only been at it fifty years or so.

"That's why your question of how long it takes to learn to be a good cowboy is hard to answer. As I said before, it all depends on the man, or the boy, how steady he stays at it and what kind of blood runs in his veins. Your age is a good age to start in, Kip, most any age from your first year till you're eighteen.

"Range riding calls for all a man's got in him and that's why the younger a feller starts the better chance he's got. The cowmen's kids have the best chance at that all around, for he's right in the thick of it all the time, where a green stranger coming into the country would have a hard time getting any kind of a job on the range, about the same as a cowboy getting a job as a clerk in some office. Some experience is what's

"The cowmen's kids have the b chance at that all around."

WillJames

needed, and a cow outfit would be a mighty fine training school but there's no time for training, every man has to know his work and there's plenty of that to do.

"I'm finally getting to answer your question, and taking things in general a whole lot I'd say that with a young feller about eighteen, and if he got the chance, he could learn to be a pretty good all around cowboy in four or five years' time, that is if he's got the makings to be one. In that time he could learn to be a pretty fair rider and roper and savvy stock and range. He'd have a good start and a steady stirrup to ride on up to more learning.

"But there's no schools to break in cowboys, and I don't know how a young feller would start in unless he had a chance like you have, Kip, because no well-run outfit will take on a tenderfoot. They can't be responsible and they have no time to watch him, and the only chance I see if a young feller wants to start in is to get in the cow country first, get some job at some farm that sometimes borders the big outfits' ranges and that way get onto the ropes of the country and the ways of working. Later on he could branch out from the farm to some little outfit and in time learn enough so he can get a job on the big outfit.

"And another thing," Uncle Bill went on, as he looked at Kip, "if you have any ambitions to be a cowboy you better sit up in your saddle." He grinned. "You're riding like a sack of corn untied in the middle."

Scootie laughed, that was another one on Kip.

But Uncle Bill handed her the same medecine. "And you too, Scootie," he says, still grinning. "You ain't riding no better."

"I ain't been wanting to tell you," he went on, "thinking you'd find out by yourselves, but it seems like neither one of you has got on to riding as yet. I had hopes that you two could sit up on a horse, not like a stick nor like a sack of potatoes but *with* your horse.

"If you ride stiff like a stick some rough horse will break your back, and if you ride like a bag of potatoes there ain't going to be many horses you can ride, not on a cow outfit." Uncle Bill was educating now more than ever, and he couldn't get over explaining the fact that they had to learn to be *with* and not against their horses' every move and not to slouch in the saddle.

"A man that's rode rough horses never slouches," he says.

"You'll both ride better next summer, and you both got an amount of learning that won't hurt you with your schooling when you get back home."

Scootie spoke up. "Why," she asked, "do you have to remind us of school when we're trying not to think of it?"

Kip backed her up on that.

"Well," says Uncle Bill, "I guess I shouldn't remind you of that, but schooling is schooling wherever you get it. You shouldn't dodge it because a little of that don't hurt anybody, all depends on your capacity and your likings. As for myself I'm happy to be a know-nothing cowboy, but I'm sure all the way for anybody who's got a chance to learn something. That's why I thought I'd remind you kids so you'll take advantage of the chance you have and not be ignorant like me.

"Of course," he went on, lying, "I won't miss you kids. I'll be shoving cattle down off one hill and up another, and I'll sure be busy. But I'll be with Uncle Frank when you two come back next summer, and I'm thinking I won't have to remind neither of you to sit up in your saddles again."

The kids sort of grinned at him, but there wasn't much smile in their grins, for they'd just realized that they'd soon be hopping on a long train and hitting back for the tall steel and concrete canyons, school books and walls.

Uncle Bill, like with the kids, sort of felt that the riding days was getting few. The old cowboy had never seen a summer go so fast, neither did Kip and Scootie, and now that there was a cloud on the skyline marking less play and more work they done their best to ride out of the shadow of it.

But the shadow came on, and it was a kind of solemn outfit that rode back to the ranch one evening, and more solemn when Uncle Frank produced a letter from the kids' mother, saying that Kip and Scootie was due to be sent back to the big city in a few days, and asking why there'd been no word as to their behavior and health and safety the last two weeks or so.

Uncle Frank sort of laughed as he showed the letter to Uncle Bill and Martha, and says, "Why in samhill are they worrying about the kids' good behavior or anything happening to 'em? . . . There's daggone little mischief they can get into here and about the worst that can happen to 'em is getting their clothes mussed up. It strikes me queer how city folks think up of so many dangerous things happening out here, like as if the whole country and everything in it was out to get a feller. If I had kids of my own I'd feel better seeing 'em crawl into a mountain lion's den that I would seeing 'em cross a street."

The kids agreed with their uncle, even if they didn't have no hankering to crawl into a mountain lion's den. Then Scootie stirred up enough interest to ask:

"But what about rattlesnakes, Uncle Frank?"

"They're not near as dangerous as some of the maniacs that's running loose in every city," he says, sort of huffed up. "A rattlesnake will most always get out of your way if it can, and it'll anyhow warn you. . . . But the West ain't the only place where there's rattlesnakes. I read in the papers every once in a while of them being found most everywhere in the United States. We have none of the big diamond back rattler here in the northwest and I read where some parts of the thickly settled eastern states have more than their share of them, and other poisonous snakes that don't rattle no warning."

That little talk on the snakes took the kids' minds off the home going subject, but it was just for a little while, and neither Uncle Frank's nor Uncle Bill's minds worked so good as to keep the talk going on that subject nor think up of another.

"Now Kip and Scootie," Uncle Frank finally went on, noticing the not too happy looks returning on their faces, "you'll be glad to see your dad and mother again, won't you? You've been away from 'em for a long time."

"Sure we'll be glad," says Kip, "but I'd be gladder if I could see them here and didn't have to leave."

"Me too," says Scootie.

Uncle Frank put his arms around the kids. "That would be better," he says, "but I don't see no way how that can be done, and you got to show a little cowboy spirit now and grin, even if the trail is a little rough, for a good cowboy never whimpers."

"And anyhow," Uncle Frank added on, "you'll be back again next summer. You know how to ride pretty good now and we'll all have a heap more fun."

"That's all right," says Kip, trying hard to keep from sniffing, "but we have a few more days yet, haven't we?"

"Yes," Martha chips in, "and you'll have to try and keep from getting your clothes all mussed up so it won't take so long to clean and pack them."

"Can't we just leave them here for next summer?" Scootie asks. "We won't need any overalls and boots in the city"—she tried to grin. "They'd only make us homesick."

Uncle Frank grinned and says, "Sure you can leave 'em here."

The kids didn't at all worry about their clothes getting mussed up in the next few days that followed. They was out riding with Uncle Bill every day or playing around the corrals with their ropes and they was sure making every minute of their last few days count.

The day before they was to leave, the riders from the line camps drifted in with their strings of saddle horses. The two riders who'd drifted on to other ranges had come back too. The hay hands had left and Uncle Frank had got word from the pool outfit for him and his riders to join the round-up in a couple of days. He'd have to start gathering his saddle horses right away to

He'd have to start gathering his saddle horses right away.

be there at that time, but on account of the kids, and not wanting to make 'em feel bad in learning of what they'd be missing by having to leave just as the fall round-up was starting, he held off gathering the horses till after they'd left and he told all hands not to say a word in front of 'em about the round-up.

But the kids had a hunch of such goings on. They stuck around the corrals and bunk house on their last day and as they came near and touched the different horses they'd rode that summer there was a lump come up their throats and they looked at one another sort of queer. It'd just come to 'em how attached they'd got to their horses, what good pardners they'd got to be in all their fun and how they'd miss them.

The time to leave come, and a heap too quick. Kip and Scootie, all dressed up in their town clothes, made the rounds at the bunk house, shook hands with the cowboys who didn't do so well acting cheerful. They shook hands with the ranch hands, the choreman, and even with the grinning chinese cook, then they went to the corrals, gave their horses a last petting and, still trying to hold up pretty brave, went to the house and kissed Martha good-bye.

The big car, with Uncle Frank and Uncle Bill in it, was drove up to the porch, the luggage was loaded, the kids climbed in and with a long look at the whole ranch, waving of hands to the cowboys standing by the bunk house and another look at the horses in the corral, the car was started and stirred a dust that soon blurred their sight.

Uncle Bill went along to the railroad with 'em, and done his best to keep a string of cheerful talk going all along the way, but that wasn't so easy to do and some of his good jokes and remarks wasn't even heard.

The kids felt near as strange in their town clothes, riding in an automobile and then getting sight of the railroad, and what there was of the town, as they did when they first begin to wear overalls and come to the big country from the big city. They hadn't been near the railroad during the whole summer, and when the train that was to take 'em away pulled in they stared at it near the same way as though they'd never seen one before.

There wasn't much time spent waiting at the depot, and it was better there wasn't because nobody felt very comfortable and what talk there was came in jerks and not in too strong a tone.

"Tell your ma and pa that they'd better come out themselves next summer," says Uncle Frank, after he'd spoke to the conductor and tipped him as to the care of the kids. "Tell 'em I said for 'em to look at you and compare their color and complexion with yours, and that if they don't come out pretty soon and shake themselves in good air and sunshine they'll be the color of the sooty gray stone walls they're living in the thick of."

"All aboard," hollers the conductor. Kip, his lower lip a-quivering but trying to smile, managed to say "good-bye" at Uncle Frank and Uncle Bill. Scootie didn't act any braver than Kip did as she said good-bye, and Uncle Bill managed to make 'em grin by grinning himself and saying:

"I'd rather you'd say 'so long' instead of good-bye. Good-bye sounds like you're going to be gone a long, long time and that ain't a fact. Christmas will soon be along and then first thing you know it'll be spring again."

Scootie jumped up, put her arms around the old cowboy's neck and kissed him. "Well, so long, Uncle Bill," she says.

The "So long" was repeated again as the train started to pull out, and when it got out of sight the two uncles looked at one another in a sort of vacant way. Uncle Bill rubbed the hand that Kip had shook over the cheek that Scootie had kissed, and with a twisted grin on his face, he says:

"Daggone their little hides . . ."